Just Add Heat

Justine can hardly believe her good fortune. She's a web star with her own cooking show and living with a sexy man. The only problem with the whole setup is that she can't remember any of it.

Luckily, her memories seem to be tied up with her hormones, and Carter is more than happy to do whatever's necessary to help her to remember.

Also included is a bonus read *A Peek Into the Mind of Carter Ross*

ISBN-13: 978-0615731698

Published by Pin-up Press

Cover Photos ©PLATEN, © artjazz Fotolia.com

For information: www.pinuppress.com.

Just Add Heat

Genevieve Jourdin

Pin-up Press

Chapter One

"Juss, wake up." I stiffened as I tried to pry my eyes open, a difficult task since they felt like they were glued together. A moment later something touched my face and it didn't feel like a Chihuahua tongue.

"Baby, come on." Crap. There was a man beside me. Or maybe I was still dreaming?

I managed to open my eyelids a crack. Green eyes were peering down at me. *This can't be good.*

"What are you doing?" I managed to croak. I couldn't believe how dry my mouth was.

"It's been two hours. How are you feeling?" He started to stroke my arm. Holy crap. What did I *do* last night?

"Two hours? What's going on?" I was able to open my eyes a bit more to see my best friend Cheryl's brother leaning over me. Her very hot, younger brother. Unfortunately, his hotness didn't make it any less icky.

"Don't you remember what happened?" His face creased into a frown.

"Uh, not really. Did we go out drinking?" Drinking seemed like the only reasonable answer.

"No. You slipped getting out of the shower and hit your head on the toilet. You wouldn't go to the hospital so Dad told me to keep an eye on you."

"Where is Cheryl?" And why wasn't *she* with me right now?

"At home. Do you want me to call her?"

What the heck was Carter doing here alone? Why would I be showering while he was here? My stomach started a slow roll. Something wasn't adding up.

"Do you want some water?" He reached over me to the night table and grabbed a glass half filled with water and some mostly melted ice cubes.

"Thanks." I took the glass and gulped a huge swallow. My mouth now felt better but I was still confused.

"Does your head hurt at all?"

"Um, I don't mean to be rude, but why are you here?"

"Where else am I supposed to be?"

I looked around the room and recognized the furniture, my furniture. We weren't at Carter's apartment, this was my room.

"Carter, this is *my* house. I think it's time

you left."

He stared at me and then his eyes widened. "Do you know your name?"

"Justine, duh. What's your problem?" I was getting a little uncomfortable now; something might be wrong with Carter. "How did you get in here?"

"I'm going to call Dad, just hang on a sec." He rolled over to the other side of the bed and picked up a phone.

"What do you think you're doing?" I hissed as I grabbed for it. "Don't call your dad. How do you think you're going to explain being here?"

He held the phone out of my reach and scooted to the edge of the bed. "Just calm down, don't get overexcited, my dad will know what to do." He sounded freaked out, and I was starting to feel the same way.

"Hey Dad, sorry to call so late, but something's wrong with Juss. She doesn't remember hitting her head and she asked me what I was doing in her house. No, she hasn't mentioned that, hold on." He turned back to me. "Are you having any trouble with your vision?"

I shook my head feeling mortified. Carter was telling Cheryl's dad he was at my house at...I looked at the bedside clock, 3:34! What was he doing here in the middle of the night? My heart started pounding. Something wasn't right. That wasn't my bedside clock. My clock had bright blue illumination so I could easily see it. This clock was round and old timey looking.

Like the ones my mom used to have. What the hell was going on?

"Okay, yeah, I'm going to bring her right now. Thanks." He looked serious.

"Dad said we should go down to the hospital. It sounds like you might have a concussion."

"I don't have a concussion. My head doesn't even hurt." I put my hand up to my head and felt around. "See? I'm fine." Right about then I hit a tender spot on my right temple. "Ahhg." A searing pain shot through my head followed by a low throb. I slouched back down onto my pillows.

"Come on, sweetie; let's get you down there so they can check you out."

I noticed he'd called me sweetie, but I let that slide since I had a bigger issue on my hands. "I am not going to the hospital, I just need some Tylenol and I'll be just fine," I panted. My ears started buzzing, a sure sign that a panic attack was coming on. I couldn't think. Suddenly I felt hands on my upper arms and then Carter's face was directly in front of me.

"Just breathe. It's okay, everything will be all right. Calm down." I knew I was about to lose it and right at this moment I was glad Carter was with me. The only problem was that he was the reason I was panicking. "I'm going to get you a cold towel. Hang on." He got up off of the bed and bolted out of the room. Seconds later he was back, holding the towel to the back of my neck.

"Okay, I'm cool." I wasn't, but it felt better to

tell him I had control of myself.

"I'm serious; we have to get to the hospital." He reached down then held out a pair of grubby runners.

"Those aren't mine."

He looked down at them and then at me. "Yes they are. You don't remember your shoes?"

I stared at them. I had never seen these shoes in my life. Had someone gotten in and somehow traded out my shoes? And my clock? That didn't even make sense.

"Come on, we have to go." He bent down and scooped me up bridal style. "You can put them on while I drive." He carried me out to the living room and grabbed some keys off of the table in the entryway. He managed to open the door, walk out, and lock up while never putting me down. The beep of a car alarm made me jump as Carter stalked over to a black truck. He popped open the door and set me in the passenger seat while I sat there like a dead fish, too freaked out to even fight what was happening. A moment later he sat down in the driver's seat before leaning over to fasten my seatbelt.

"It'll be okay, Juss." He gave my hand a squeeze and I fought the urge to pull away. It hurt if I tried to think too hard, so I just stared out the front window and tried to stay calm. In no time we were pulling up to the hospital. I'd never been to a hospital in the middle of the night before. It was lit up and shadowed, with hardly any cars in the parking lot. Surreal.

Carter pulled into a spot close to the entrance of the ER, picked me up again and closed the door with his hip. Before I realized it, we were in the building and facing a mean-looking nurse in a room half-filled with dejected looking people. "Excuse me; I have a head injury here."

"Okay, fill these out and I'll we'll be right with you." She handed Carter a clipboard with a pen on a chain. "I'll go get a chair." She turned and walked away as I sat there with my hands wrapped around Carter's neck. It was almost like all of this was happening to someone else.

He found a seat in the middle of the room, leaving me on his lap. He moved the clipboard to his left hand and started filling out the forms while I watched idly. He had beautiful hands. And beautiful fingers. Hmm. This was the shiniest floor ever. *I wonder what they use on it?* Suddenly, the nurse was in front of me with a wheelchair.

"Let's get you in here and see what's what." The nurse had a kind voice that didn't match her face.

As he set me in the chair I heard a familiar voice. "Justine, how are you feeling?" I looked over to see Cheryl's dad, Robert. I felt a strange sense of calm mixed with dread because he had a concerned look on his face. Luckily, Cheryl's dad was an Ob/Gyn, and I knew he was often at the hospital at odd hours. It made me feel a lot better to have someone I knew here. "Well, okay I guess. Carter woke me up, then he called you." I was too embarrassed to tell Robert that Carter was in my bed. He might think we had sex or something. "I'm sorry he dragged you down here. I really don't know what's going on with him."

"Don't worry about that. I had a delivery to attend to a couple of hours ago. I'm glad Carter caught me before I left. Let's go into the exam room so we can check things out." He turned and walked to a room right off of the lobby. I started rolling that way and turned to see Carter was pushing me. Strangely, I had gotten over my earlier panic and now I was freakishly accepting of Carter being with me.

"Justine, why don't you sit up here on the table and let me get a look at you until an ER doctor is free."

Carter helped me up onto a table covered with crinkly paper. I scooted up so that my legs were dangling off the side. Robert picked something up and pointed it at my face. A second later a blinding light pierced my eyeball.

"Ow. That's too bright." He moved to the other eye with similar results. After that, everything was a blur. I know I was x-rayed and prodded, but I really wasn't paying much attention. I was so drowsy. All I wanted was to go back to sleep.

The next thing I knew, I was opening my

eyes to a hospital room. I felt a whole lot better than I had when I had fallen asleep. To my right, Carter was slumped on a chair. Why was he still here? I needed to call Cheryl. Why wasn't she here with me? I sat up looking for my purse. I needed my phone but it wasn't anywhere I could see.

"Can I get you something?" Carter's voice made me jerk my head in his direction.

"I really need my phone. I want to call Cheryl."

"I'm sorry; I left your bag at home. I already called Cheryl, though. She'll be here a little later. Do you want to use mine?"

"Carter, why are you here? Why were you at my house in the middle of the night? God, I don't even remember last night." Thinking about that stirred my feelings of anxiety and I realized something was very wrong.

"I love you, where else would I be? Obviously, I'll stay until we find out you're all right."

He loves me? Okay, now I was sure something was wrong. Cheryl's brother was telling me he loved me. We didn't have that kind of relationship. Cheryl was more like a sister to me than a friend, and I guess you could call the feelings I had for Carter brotherly, but this was just weird.

"Carter, you're freaking me out. Don't tell me you love me. That's just weird. Why were you at my house last night?" Maybe something was wrong with *Carter*. Yeah, that would make more sense.

"What are you talking about? Of course I love you. We live together." He had gotten up to stand by me and took my hand off of the bed. I couldn't help it, I jerked it away.

I could see the shock and hurt in Carter's eyes but I didn't care. "Don't say that. We don't live together. Are you crazy? You. Don't. Live. With. Me." I enunciated each word clearly so that he could understand.

"I'm calling the doctor. Just calm down." He turned and left the room. I didn't know what to think of what Carter had just said. I think I would know if I was involved with Carter. Like that could ever happen. Sure, he looked good, but I had known him since he was fourteen. He was Cheryl's little brother, so he was four years younger than me. There was no way I would ever get involved with him, *there wasn't*. Anyway, I wasn't ready to jump back into the dating pool; I had just dumped the cheating scumbag, John. It hadn't even been two months yet. I really needed to talk to Cheryl.

Just then the door opened and a doctor I didn't recognize came in with Carter on his heels. "Carter, could I please have some privacy?" He stopped and looked at the doctor before nodding at me and turning around. Once he was gone and the door was shut I looked to the doctor. "I'm sorry about him, he's my best friend's brother." I shrugged to let him know

9

that Carter's behavior was no reflection on me.

The doctor gave me a funny look and wrote something down on a clipboard.

"Do you know what day it is, Justine?" Huh?

He was looking serious. "Um, Thursday, yeah, Thursday. My movie was due back yesterday and I dropped it off before I went grocery shopping." Whew. It felt good to remember something.

"Do you know what month it is?"

"July." Okay, easy questions.

"Do you know what year it is?"

"2010." What kind of inane questions were these?

He paused as if trying to find the right words. "Justine, I'm afraid you might have a slight case of amnesia. Do you remember last night at all? Falling and hitting your head?" He was frowning, never a good sign.

"Amnesia? No, I don't have amnesia, doctor. I don't remember falling or hitting my head." My hand automatically went to my temple and I felt the spot that hurt earlier. Wow. There was a lump there. What the heck happened last night?

"Justine, it's 2012. It's September 2012. You had an accident last night and hit your head in the bathroom. Your friend outside brought you in because you were confused and agitated. I know it's hard but you need to relax and let your body heal. You'll feel a lot better as soon as the swelling on your brain goes down."

Holy crap! 2012? How could it be 2012? My

brain was swollen? Two years of my life were gone? I couldn't believe it. There had to be some mistake.

"Are you sure?" I looked around the room for any sign of the date. Unfortunately, there was no handy calendar hanging on the walls, just ugly pinstriped wallpaper. If only I had my phone.

"I'm sure, Justine. I'm going to order some tests, but I'll go get your friend to come sit with you."

He went to the door and stepped out. I had amnesia? How could that be? *That's soap opera crap.* I tried to gather myself. I needed all my wits about me for this. When the door opened it wasn't the doctor coming, it was Carter. He looked ashen. Freakishly hot, but ashen.

"Carter, tell me the truth. Is it 2012? Give me your phone." He held it out and I snatched it up. It took a second to make my shaking fingers work, but finally the screen came to life. September 29, 2012. No way!

"Yes. Listen, I called your mom, she'll be here in a couple of hours. She's leaving right now. Cheryl will be here soon, too. Your neurologist is setting up some more tests and said he'd be right back. Is there anything I can get for you?"

He was looking at me earnestly. I didn't know what to say to him. "You said we lived together? As roommates or..." I couldn't finish the sentence. I couldn't even finish the thought.

It seemed all wrong. Surely he couldn't mean we *lived* together. With sex and ...stuff. I would definitely remember that.

"We've been living together for almost seven months as a *couple*. We've been together for about a year and a half. About as long as Just Add Heat."

"Just add heat? How did we get together? I hardly ever spend any time with you." The questions were all garbled in my mind. I didn't know what to ask first.

"You write a food blog. It's very popular. You try foods at restaurants then dissect them, recreate them by spicing them up, and post recipes and video, but with a sexy spin. That's what we were going to do last night; you wanted to try out the Thai place for new dishes." He didn't answer me about our supposed relationship, I noticed.

"What about my job? Did anyone call them and tell them I'm in here? I think I'm supposed to work tonight." Thursday nights were busy. This was a bad night to be out.

"Justine, the website is your job. You haven't worked at the restaurant for more than a year. When you started getting popular, you started making enough on advertising to quit your job and do the site full time. You also do a web show. Right now you're working on a cookbook." He looked at me for some sign of recognition. Nope.

Wait. I haven't worked at the restaurant for

a year? Oh god. Maybe I really did have amnesia. I was finally in charge of my own kitchen, I would never *quit*. I was starting to hyperventilate. I'm writing a cookbook? That was actually kind of cool if only I could remember it. But wait, back to the important stuff.

"We've been together for a year and a half? *Together* together? How did that happen? No offence but, you're young. Too young. You're just out of school."

"I finished college two and a half years ago. I'm a graphic artist at Webster and James, the advertising firm. We started going out last April, after we spent time setting up your website and getting it off the ground. You came to me for some help with the layout. Do you remember that at all?"

I shook my head. Didn't ring a bell. Nope. I couldn't really see myself doing something on the internet. I'm a chef, a damn good one. That just didn't seem like me. Going out with a younger guy didn't seem like me either. Well, not Cheryl's brother, at least. That would be too bizarre. Yucky even.

He sighed but didn't say anything. We just sat there, staring at each other and not talking. I didn't know what to say, what to ask. I could tell that I was going to go to pieces soon. Nothing was adding up. I didn't recognize that life as mine.

There was a tap on the door and Cheryl

breezed in smiling. "I fed Lucy, she gobbled up everything, I also fed Fred and Ethel since I wasn't sure when Carter was going to go back home. Are you feeling okay?"

"Cheryl." I was relieved to have some familiarity. "What did you do to your hair?" It was in shoulder length waves. Cheryl had a sleek bob that was at her chin. Hair doesn't grow overnight.

She peered at me strangely. "It's been like this forever. We were just talking about that the other day, remember? We were going through those magazines to find a new style."

I was shaking my head when Carter interjected. "She has some kind of amnesia. She thinks it's 2010. She doesn't remember her website or last night or me." Carter looked defeated and said that last sentence in a low tone I could barely hear.

"Amnesia? Oh my god! What do you last remember?" Cheryl's eyes had widened outrageously. "You don't remember your site? Oh my god, that's your life! You don't remember Carter? You *live* with him. How many fingers am I holding up?" Cheryl thrust three fingers at my face.

"Cheryl, I'm not blind, I just can't remember some stuff right now." I scrunched back on the bed and Cheryl withdrew her hand.

"This is really freaky, Juss. How can you not remember Carter? You spend practically every free moment with him." That made me squirm in my bed. It didn't seem right to be talking about this with Cheryl. I felt embarrassed to be connected with her younger brother. I mutely shook my head again.

"Carter, can I have a minute alone with your sister?" He nodded and left the room. "Cheryl, I'm losing it right now. I'm not dating your brother, there has to be some mistake. I can't process the fact that I am missing two years of my life. What is going on? Carter said I don't work at the restaurant anymore. Why would I quit? Help me! I don't know what to do." All my words were running together as I poured my heart out to Cheryl. Cheryl with longer hair. Oh god, oh god, I needed a Xanax. I could feel my panic attack coming on in earnest now. There was going to be no stopping it. My chest was pounding and I was gasping for air.

"Oh shit. Hold on, Juss." She pressed a button on the railing of my bed. "Could someone please come in here? I think Justine is having an anxiety attack."

"Someone will be right in." The disembodied voice came from a tiny box next to the button. I noticed this through the haze of my terror. It felt like my heart was beating out of my chest. *I'm having a heart attack. Thank goodness I was in a hospital.*

The door burst open and a nurse wearing flowered scrubs came into my room. She walked up to my bed and checked something beside me. It was some kind of monitor connected to my arm and finger and I hadn't even noticed it before.

"Take a deep breath and try to calm down. The doctor will be with you in just a moment." She messed with something and wrote something down on my chart.

"I really need a Xanax. I have some in my purse."

"I'm sorry, Justine, you can't have any medications until I know what's going on with your brain." The doctor from earlier walked in while answering my plea. "You're just having some anxiety right now, no one could blame you. You've had a huge shock. Just try to relax and we'll get you fixed up in no time."

Easier said than done, but I tried to get a hold on my breathing. It was the only thing I could manage right now. I closed my eyes and took a few deep breaths. It didn't help my heart rate, but at least I felt a tiny bit more in control. A minute later I felt a cool wetness across my face and I opened my eyes. Carter had come back in and was holding a towel. He then stuck it behind my neck and I felt a little better almost at once.

"Thank you." I reached up to touch the towel and met Carter's fingers. They were cold. "Thank you," I repeated while looking up at him. It felt strange but also somehow familiar. At this point I would take familiarity wherever I could get it.

Chapter Two

After I got over my panic attack, I didn't have a moment to myself to think. Before I could even get my bearings, an orderly came in with another wheelchair to take me for testing. I don't know why they had to wheel me there, I could walk perfectly fine. I walked from the bed to the chair with no mishap, anyway.

I was hoping that I would have some kind of breakthrough while I was in the CT scanning machine. I didn't. Nothing was clear to me. I know I have a Chihuahua named Lucy. I got her as soon as I graduated from culinary school. She was a rescue, so I didn't know how old she was, but earlier Cheryl said she stopped by my house and fed her, so at least I knew she's doing okay. Cheryl said she fed someone else, but I was so freaked out by that time that I didn't question her and now she wasn't here. Maybe I got another dog or possibly a cat. I always felt guilty leaving Lucy alone for such long shifts at the restaurant. But evidently I don't work at Heavenly Vegetables anymore, so I didn't have a clue.

I was relieved when I got back to the room and found it empty. I wasn't ready to deal with what I had learned today. Dr. Turner said I was suffering from retrograde amnesia. He wasn't sure why I couldn't remember the last two years. I wondered the same thing. Did something happen that was so awful my mind was blocking it out? If so, it's got to be really bad. It probably had to do with Carter. That's what made the most sense to me.

Now that everything was quiet, I could think about Carter. Okay, he looks good, that's obvious. His eyes are the same dark green as Cheryl's (I was so jealous), plus he's tall and built like a swimmer. His black hair is a little long, but he dressed a lot better than I do, at least from what I can remember about him. That was the big problem. I don't really know. I mean, I only know him as Cheryl's brother. Of course we've hung out lots of times, but Cheryl was always there. I couldn't think of a single time that Carter and I had spent any time alone.

Cheryl's been my best friend since freshman year of college when we lived across the hall from each other in the same dorm. We gravitated towards each other since we each had roommates we didn't get along with. Well, Cheryl didn't get along with her roommate. My roommate was a psycho and I tried to avoid spending time in my room while she was awake. Cheryl and I moved into one of her parents' rental houses our junior year, and the rest was history. We lived together with her boyfriend Paulo until a few years ago when I bought my fixer-upper on the East Side.

Hmm. I guess it's been like five years now. I didn't want to think about that. I didn't know the person I'm supposed to be now. On the plus side, I don't seem to have aged much. I know because when I went to the bathroom earlier I looked hard at myself. I was shocked at first; my hair was so dark it was almost black. The last time I remember dyeing it, it was red. I was happy to see that my bangs, a horrible error in judgment, had finally grown out. I was also more pale than usual so my dark eyes stood out, but all in all I was relieved to see I looked pretty much the same.

But back to Carter. I didn't know what to feel. He wasn't here when I got back to my room and I was happy for the reprieve. I had no clue what to do there. I don't love him in a romantic way. He's great—he's Cheryl's brother. I've known him for years and he's fun to be around and everything, but we were never *intimate*. Sure, he grew up to be hot as hell and he's also quite possibly the most polite and gentlemanly person I've ever met next to Cheryl's dad, Robert, but he's still Cheryl's little brother. I just couldn't wrap my head around the fact that we were a couple. *Too weird.*

This was *all* too strange. I didn't even know what's in my refrigerator right now. A simple thing really, but it's a big deal if you can't remember. At least for me. I don't like change. I need to know what's what all the time. I realize it probably had something to do with the chaotic way I was raised. I didn't even need therapy to understand that, but right now I felt like my world had been turned upside down. That's why I couldn't bring myself to believe I was involved with Carter. How could he go from being Cheryl's little brother to my *boyfriend*? Was that even the right term? Is it live-in lover? No, I don't like the sound of that. Anyway, the point is that he's four years younger than me. He's only twenty three; I know because I made the food for his birthday party a few months back. I'm almost twenty eight. Wait, I was almost twenty eight *two years ago*. I'm twenty nine now. No, it's September and my birthday is in August, I'm *thirty*. The big 3-0.

I had to stop thinking. It wasn't helping, it only made my chest tight. I wanted to go to sleep and wake up and have everything be normal.

I don't know how long I had been staring at the ceiling before the door opened and the nurse from earlier came back in. She smiled and walked over to the machine at the side of my bed. She nodded as she jotted down something then turned to me.

"Are you feeling okay?" Hmm. Physically, I guess I felt all right. My stomach growled. When did I eat last?

"Yeah. I'm pretty hungry, though. Can I get something to eat?"

"Yes." She looked down at her watch. "The lunch cart should be around shortly," she answered and went to a chair over by the door with a newspaper sitting on it. I hadn't noticed it before or I would have already looked through it. "It's from yesterday, but at least you'll be able to get some current information from it." She handed me the paper and I pored over the headlines.

Nothing good stared back at me. We're still in a recession, still in Afghanistan. Everything looked about the same.

I scanned the top of the paper. Yep, September 28, 2012. I flopped back on the pillow and closed my eyes. I just wanted to rest my brain. I was totally not ready to deal with this yet. A few seconds later I heard the rattle of the lunch cart down the hall and the click of my door, sleep would have to wait.

"Honey, are you feeling better?" It was my mother, not my lunch. I braced myself for any possible surprises before I opened my eyes.

"Yeah Mom, I'm feeling a lot better. Thanks for coming." She had added some blonde highlights to her hair since I had seen her last but, I didn't notice anything drastic.

"Well, Carter called and told me you had an

accident so I just hopped in the car and got on the road. You look okay, though, besides the bruise on the side of your face." She sounded almost disappointed that I wasn't wrapped in bandages and in traction.

"I *am* having a bit of a problem. Evidently, I've got some sort of amnesia."

She looked at me like I was kidding at first. A second later she looked aghast. "Amnesia, what do you mean? You know who *I* am. What have you forgotten?"

"The last two years, apparently. I don't remember anything after 2010."

She just sat there with a strange look on her face as I struggled to find something to say. We didn't have a bosom buddy type relationship like some mothers and daughters do. We pretty much left each other alone until the holidays or some crisis. Well, here's a crisis. *Crap.* Unfortunately, she just didn't have it in her to make me feel better. Thankfully, I heard the cart stop outside the door. An orderly (well, I guess he was an orderly, he didn't look old enough to have gone through any kind of medical training) poked his head in.

He smiled at me and he looked so hilarious in his hairnet that I couldn't resist grinning back at him. "You didn't fill out your lunch card this morning. Do you want meatloaf or the broiled cod?"

I preferred not to eat meat, but I wasn't a strict vegetarian. "Cod, please." He went to the cart and brought over a tray that had a dish covered with a plastic dome, a little milk carton like you get in elementary school, and a pudding cup. Wow, they go all out at Austin General.

"Thanks." He left and I started in on my food so that I didn't have to speak to my mother. It was surprisingly good.

"So I guess you don't remember that I got divorced from Bill last year, huh?" Oh yeah, my mom was still sitting in the chair. I looked up at this new revelation.

"You divorced Bill? Why?" Bill was actually a good guy. This hit me out of left field. I took another bite of my carrots; they needed seasoning. As I waited for my mother to answer me I ripped open the tiny salt packet and it spilled over the entire plate. Dang it.

"I just got tired of all the boredom. He never wanted to go out and do anything. He wanted to stay home and work in the yard." She said it like it was a crime. Poor Bill was on the road for years as a medical device salesman and finally, when he gets a chance to be at home, my mother dumps him?

I threw my arm over my eyes. I really couldn't deal with this right now. Why had Carter called her? Things must have seemed pretty dire this morning.

"Hi there, Carter. It's nice to see you again." Mom's voice pulled me out of my thoughts. I moved my arm so that I could see him. The door was still open from the lunch delivery so I hadn't heard him come in. My stomach flipped over. Wow, I hadn't felt the butterflies since high school.

"Hello Gloria. How was your drive?" He leaned down and gave her a kiss on the cheek. He was only being polite but it grated on my nerves. I didn't even realize they knew each other.

"It was long. They're working on the highway again. I just want to relax and get something to eat." She looked over at my lunch and scrunched up her nose. Uh, I'm lying over here in a *hospital* bed suffering from some kind of head trauma. I hated the way she tried to make everything about herself.

Carter walked past her and up to me. "Any change?" he asked me hopefully.

"No." His face fell and I felt a little guilty for not remembering what he obviously wanted me to. It still felt strange, but I felt more comfortable with Carter than with my own mother. *How screwed up is that?*

"It'll come." He squeezed my hand and I looked down. I didn't want to see the disappointment that I couldn't do anything about.

"Carter, what have you been up to?" my mother asked. I must have made some kind of face because he squeezed my hand again.

"I'm sorry," he mouthed silently before he turned to my mother. "Work's been busy and Justine's cookbook is coming along great." He looked over at me.

I shook my head. Sorry, still don't recall anything about it. I wanted to ask him questions about us, about me, but I didn't want to do that in front of my mother. I was about to suggest she go down to the cafeteria when Cheryl's dad walked in.

"Justine, how are you feeling this morning? Dr. Turner filled me in on your problem." He walked around to the other side of my bed so I turned my attention to him.

I didn't know how to answer him. I was feeling lost. I was feeling scared. Did he want the truth? "Fine," I lied.

He looked into my eyes. "You're looking better than last night. Give it time." My throat felt thick and my eyes started to tear up. Robert patted my hand and exchanged a look with Carter, before turning to Mom.

"Gloria, it's a pleasure to see you again. I was going to have a cup of coffee, would you care to join me?" It was like Robert could read my mind.

"That would be great. I was just telling Carter I could use a bite to eat." She got up and grabbed her huge purse which was on the floor beside her. "I'll be back in a little while, Justine."

I smiled and lifted my hand in a weak wave and she and Robert left the room.

"I'm sorry about that. I was so worried about you this morning that I felt I had to call her. She *is* your mother."

"It's okay; you couldn't know how she would be."

"Well, yes, I did, but I called her anyway." He shook his head ruefully. "Maybe Dad will keep her busy." He stood there in silence for a moment and I forced myself to speak.

"Can I ask you something?" He nodded. "Do I have a cat?"

"No." He didn't say anything else; he just looked at me like I had a head injury.

"Carter, I need to ask you something else." I gathered up my courage.

"Anything."

"Do I love you?" He looked as if I slapped him.

"Yes." It was barely a whisper. My throat constricted. I knew he would say that, but it seemed like it was physically hurting him. I wanted to comfort him, and apologize for not loving him now, but I couldn't say anything. I felt frozen. I was terrified. I swallowed around the lump in my throat.

"Yes, you love me, and I love you. You are the best thing that has ever happened to me." I could hear the conviction in his voice, so I knew that he was telling me the truth, but I wasn't feeling it in my heart.

Chapter Three

Carter left when my mother came back. I was conflicted. On the one hand I needed time to myself to come to terms with my situation, to try to remember something. On the other hand, I felt like asking him to stay with me. Of course I didn't because, in truth, I didn't have much to say to him. I wanted to ask him questions, but Cheryl was the better choice to fill me in.

Anyway, he left me with my mother and she didn't have anything helpful to offer me. She knew nothing about my day to day life. She did know that I live with Carter, though, and that didn't seem fair. She hardly knows anything about me but she still knew more than I did.

She sat with me for about an hour; until I told her I was okay, and that she should go on home, back to Waco. I felt a little bad that she had driven all this way, but I got over it when she started talking about her vacation to

Orlando last summer. Really, I just didn't care, especially right now. She wasn't giving me anything to work with concerning *my* life. It wasn't like I was at Disneyworld with her and would remember something.

Shortly after she left, Dr. Turner came in and told me that I could go home tomorrow as long as I wasn't getting dizzy or anything. I was happy and petrified in equal measure. Sure, I wanted to leave the hospital, who wants to be here? Alas, I wasn't ready to go home and face— I don't know what.

After my freakishly early dinner tray was finished, Cheryl showed up. I felt like it had been forever since I had seen her, but it was really just this morning. I needed to be around someone familiar, someone who I recognized as being a part of my life.

"Hey girl," she sang as she strolled in with a purple duffle bag over her shoulder. "I brought you some pajamas and your toothbrush and stuff."

Ah, wonderful Cheryl, thinking about things I hadn't even given a thought to. Now I could brush my teeth and get out of this super thin hospital gown. I smiled as I opened the bag but it quickly faded as I stared at the contents in confusion. I didn't recognize any of the items in there. I pulled out the toiletry bag and unzipped it. I didn't even recognize my toothbrush. I was pretty sure that my toothbrush was one of those spin brushes from the grocery store, but this one was some kind of high tech device that I couldn't see myself buying. There was also a lotion I wasn't familiar with. I was happy to see that I still used Colgate and Secret, but that was pretty much it.

I reached in and pulled out my pajamas, a matching set, and a pair of green boy-shorts panties. I looked at her, wondering where she got this from. I usually slept in baggy men's boxers and worn oversized tee shirts.

"They're yours. I got everything from your house. Carter even put your purse in here since he forgot to get it last night." She reached in and pulled out a square bag of orange leather. I couldn't identify it as mine, but it looked like something I would have.

"Is Carter at my house?" I wasn't sure how I felt about letting him just hang out at my house when I wasn't there. He might be snooping through the closets or something. What if he found my vibrator?

"Yeah, he wanted to come back to the hospital but he didn't want to overwhelm you. I told him I would bring this over for you so that we could have a little girl time." She sat down on the side of my bed. I needed to know so much, but I didn't know where to start.

"So um, what's been going on the last couple of years?" I felt foolish for asking such an inane question, but I honestly felt like I had been on an extended vacation and had lost touch with everyone back home.

"Well, where do you want to start? What's the last thing you remember?"

"Let's see, it's July and I work at Heavenly Vegetables, I broke up with John, that douche, and you and Paulo had just gotten engaged." I gasped and looked at Cheryl's finger. Yep, there was a wedding band nestled beside her engagement ring.

"Oh my god, Cheryl, I missed your wedding!" I was appalled. "I'm so sorry. Congratulations." I didn't know what else to say. She leaned forward and squeezed me into a hug.

"You didn't miss it, honey. You were my maid of honor. Hold on a second." She slid off of the bed and over to the tote bag she called a purse. After a few seconds she came back to the bed and pulled out a little square frame attached to her keys. She pressed a button and pictures started flashing across the screen. She flipped through a few and then stopped. "Here, this is us at the wedding."

Sure enough, there she was looking luminous in a white gown and there I was in a navy blue dress looking happy and at ease. She flipped to the next shot and there were Carter and Paulo in tuxes on either side of me, smiling at the camera in some sort of group hug. My chest tightened. How could I not remember such a wonderful moment? How could I forget my best friend's most important day? I continued to go through the photos, pausing at one of Carter standing behind me with his arms around my waist. My heart pounded in my ears.

"When was your wedding?"

"June 18th of last year. 2011." Over a year ago. What else had I missed? I kept flipping through the pictures until I came back to where I started. I felt odd and strangely disassociated with the images I saw on the screen. That smiling woman in those shots wasn't me. They were of someone who didn't exist yet, like a Justine of the Future. I handed the photo frame back to Cheryl.

"Why did I quit my job? I love it." I did love being the executive chef at Heavenly Vegetables. I got to cook the kind of food I loved and I was finally in control of my own kitchen. I couldn't fathom why I would have thrown that away.

"You didn't love it when you quit. The new manager was a dick and didn't let you make any decisions. You actually hated working there by the end. It was a blessing your website took off. Plus, now you're kind of famous!" She was beaming at me, but I was reeling. My dream job had turned sour? That sucked.

"What do you mean I'm kind of famous?" That was something I hadn't heard before.

"Well, you do these web shows on cooking and you have a huge following. Last year one of your clips went viral and you got over a million hits. That's why you got the offer for the cookbook." I do a cooking show. That had always been my dream when I was younger. I used to do pretend cooking shows when Cheryl and I moved into the house—obviously when Cheryl wasn't home. Granted, my show was on the internet, but still. My life didn't sound so bad.

There was something else I needed to ask, but I didn't know how to broach the subject. I felt hesitant to ask Cheryl, but there was someone alone in my house. I had to do it.

"I need to know about Carter, Cheryl. I mean, the last thing I remember about Carter was the night he was over at your house for pizza and we watched a movie. How is it that we're supposedly together now?" I felt uncomfortable talking to her about Carter. Surely she thought it was weird that I was having a relationship with her younger brother. *I* felt weird about it. I just couldn't see myself as the older woman in a relationship. I was always drawn to older men. How could something that fundamental about myself change?

"Maybe you should be talking to Carter about this, Juss. Honestly, I didn't know you were together at first, I found out accidentally." I couldn't believe I hadn't told Cheryl about my love life. We shared *everything*.

"Accidentally? What, did you walk in on us having sex or something?" I joked. Cheryl raised her eyebrow at me and I cringed. "Really?"

She nodded. "It was a shock, let me tell you. I wanted to bleach my eyes, but I don't think that would have helped. It is forever seared into my brain." She was smiling but I could feel my face flush in mortification.

I didn't know what to say. I couldn't explain myself because I had no recollection of that happening. Maybe talking to Cheryl about this was a bad idea after all. There was still the problem of Carter at my house, though.

"So, um, Carter said we live together?" I asked hesitatingly. I still couldn't accept that it was true. I had dated John for over a year and I never considered moving in with him. I still felt the sting of betrayal about John. Even now, months later, I couldn't believe he had been cheating on me with my line cook, Laura. I had introduced them when we had gone out for drinks one night. To my knowledge they had never seen each other again, but how wrong I was. I still had to work with that bitch, but luckily she knew better than to throw attitude at me in my own kitchen. It suddenly occurred to me that I didn't work there anymore. I had to remember that. This day was giving me more than I could absorb.

"Yes, he moved into your house sometime in the middle of February. I know because it was super cold that day we were lugging his stuff over and I was wearing the new coat I had gotten for myself for Valentine's Day." She nodded to herself. "Yep, it was the first time I had worn it." Cheryl had always been able to recall dates by wardrobe.

So it was true. Carter lived in my house. I had no idea what I was going to do tomorrow when I got home. Could I ask him to stay somewhere else until things got back to normal? I didn't think I would feel comfortable with him staying with me before I got my memories back.

It would be different if he were a girl or maybe an ugly guy, but as I've mentioned before, young or not, he is *hot*. This wouldn't be much of a problem for most women, but, due to a genetic anomaly, hot guys turned me stupid. I became a stuttering idiot, incapable of holding an intelligent conversation for more than a few minutes at a time.

Usually this was not a problem with Carter because a) we were never really alone when we would see each other, and b) I never looked on him as someone to impress. Seriously, he's just Cheryl's younger brother.

"I'm freaking out, Cheryl." I was finally about to break down. "I don't know *anything* right now. I don't know what I do, what I wear," I pointed at the pajamas, "Nothing. I don't even know who I'm in a relationship with. I don't know what to do." I started crying, I just couldn't help it. Actually, I couldn't believe I hadn't before now.

"God Juss, I'm sorry. I guess I didn't realize how you were feeling. I know you must be terrified. I would be." She leaned over and hugged me tight. "I'll do whatever you need. Do you want to come and stay with Paulo and me? I can rearrange some things at work and we can spend our time trying to help you remember."

Cheryl was a party planner, so she worked for herself, but she was good, so she was always busy. I wanted to say yes, to go to Cheryl's house and let her take care of me while I got my bearings, but I didn't want to mess up her schedule. Even more importantly, something inside of me was telling me I needed to be home, around my own things.

"Thanks, but I think I need to be at home, sleeping in my own bed and cooking in my own kitchen. I hope just being in my house, surrounded by all of my stuff will jar something. I don't understand why this is happening to me. Why would my mind block out two years of my life?" Luckily, after my short outburst, my tears slowed down to a slow trickle.

"I don't know. You haven't told me about anything bad happening recently. Things have been going really well for you. You've been working flat out on the cookbook, but you've been nothing but excited about it. I'm pretty sure things with Carter are going smoothly too. You gripe about his neatnik tendencies, but on the whole, you guys are great together."

I pondered this for a moment. I'm working hard on my *book*. Ooh, the thought of that gave me a tingle. I'm also living with some kind of neat freak. How the hell had that happened? I was not a slave to housework. I keep a spotless kitchen, but a little clutter here and there in the rest of the house? I couldn't be bothered. Strange.

Still, there had to be something that's so horrible my mind couldn't handle it. If Cheryl didn't know what happened, who could I ask? Okay, I needed to calm down. I might wake up in the morning with my memories intact. I was stressing myself out for nothing. Everything would be fine in the morning. I just needed to get through tonight.

"The doctor is springing me tomorrow. Is there any way you can get me some clothes to go home in? I don't know where my clothes are. I don't even know what I was wearing when I came here last night."

"I'm way ahead of you. I packed you jeans and a tee shirt, and Carter said your sneakers and a hoodie are in the closet." She walked over to the little cupboard to check. "Yep, and I guess this is what you were wearing when you were admitted." She lifted up a plastic bag that I could see clothing through.

"Okay, good. I hate to ask, but could you come pick me up tomorrow? I didn't drive here so I don't have wheels."

"Uh, I think Carter is coming to get you. At least that's what the plan was, but if you want me to pick you up I will." She walked back over to the bed and sat back down. "Whatever you need."

"Oh, well if he's already planning to come, I guess that will be all right." I would probably be fine in the morning and want to have my boyfriend pick me up. Or at least Cheryl's brother. I mean, I would accept a ride from him if my car broke down and he was the only person I could get in touch with. Yeah, it would be okay.

Cheryl looked at her watch and groaned. "I need to get home and get ready for the Jameson christening tomorrow. I still have the commemorative photo boxes to finish." She made a face. "The kid is only two months old, how many important photos could he have?" She shook her head and stood up. "Is there anything else I can get for you before I leave?"

"No, I'm just going to shower and go to sleep. Thanks for coming by to visit and bringing me all this."

"My pleasure. You get a good night's rest, and I'll come by your house tomorrow after the christening. Love you." She leaned over to hug me and left.

I could only do what I said, shower and sleep. This crazy day would probably be a funny story after I got my memory back tomorrow. Fingers crossed.

Chapter Four

I opened my eyes slowly. I knew I was still in the hospital because I had had a horrible night. I had never appreciated the amount of noise and constant activity that went on in these places. My head only had a dull ache, mostly due to the fact that I'm a side sleeper and I woke up on my right side, my injury side.

The room was still semi-dark. There was only gray light filtering through the window where the sliding curtain was left unfastened. I could hear the early morning bustle of the nurses down the hallway. I didn't want to face the day because I immediately realized that my memory had not returned. I was still a twenty seven year old chef in a thirty year old blogger's body.

My heart started pounding again. That was getting old. I was going to be going home in a few hours if everything checked out. I needed to get it together.

I focused on my orange purse lying on the

chair next to the bed. I still hadn't gone through it like I planned to last night. Maybe it would trigger something and my mind would fast forward to the present. It was worth a try.

I hoisted myself into a seated position, relieved to notice no dizziness, and reached over for my bag. The first thing I spotted was my phone. It was like my old phone, but slightly different.

I touched the phone button. My first favorite contact was Carter. My stomach clenched. My second contact was Carter Work. Well, I guess that answered that question. I obviously called him a lot. I kept scrolling. Cheryl, Paulo. I went to my regular contacts and saw restaurants, my doctor, Mom, Elisa, Candace. I didn't know any Elisa or Candace. Total blank. I exited back out, noticing screens of apps I didn't recognize. I didn't want to look through my phone anymore. It was alien to me. It was all alien to me.

I dug around my purse. Ah, my wallet. Hmm, it's a really nice wallet if I do say so myself. I snapped it open and the first thing I saw was my driver's license. I had taken a new picture and I looked like a dork. Great. Credit card, credit card, library card, wow, they changed up the library cards. I opened the money compartment. Fourteen dollars and some change. That's about right; I guess I'm not rich in my new life. *That sucks*. I closed my wallet and dove back into the bag. TicTacs, hairbrush, three pens, grocery store receipts, keys, Tylenol, a scratch off lottery ticket, hey, I won three bucks, cool. That's it. Nothing to make me have a revelation. I grabbed the box of mints and shook a few into my mouth before tossing the bag aside.

I sat there, wallowing in self-pity until a nurse walked in. This was a new nurse, but she seemed friendly enough.

"How are you feeling this morning, Justine?" She knew my name. Duh, of course she did, it's on my chart.

"Pretty good," I responded. "I still don't remember anything." I figured I had better get that out there first thing. Maybe there was something they could do for me today.

"Don't try to force it, it will come when it's ready," she said wisely, as if she gets patients with amnesia several times a week.

"Yeah, that's what they say." I chewed up my TicTacs while she disconnected the pulse monitor from my finger. "When do I get to leave?"

"Well, first you can eat some breakfast, and then I'm sure the doctor is going to want to have a look at you. Do you have someone coming to pick you up?"

"Yes." I remembered Carter would be here to take me home. I never spoke to him after he left yesterday afternoon, so I didn't know what time he'd get here. I should call him. Maybe I'd wait until later. I didn't know what time I'd be released.

She left and I went to brush my teeth, the mints weren't helping my morning breath. I turned on the light and gasped.

The side of my head was bruised down to my cheek. It looked much worse than yesterday. I lightly touched all around the lump. It only hurt when I pressed near my temple. Luckily it didn't feel as bad as it looked.

After cleaning my teeth, I pulled my hair back with a brown scrunchie so that it didn't look like a squirrel's nest then crawled back into the bed and used the remote to make the back of it move up higher. When I was propped up, I looked around for something to do. Television was out. The thought of turning it on and watching some inane early morning show was loathsome. I searched around for something to read. There were no magazines or books, not even the newspaper from yesterday. What I wouldn't give for a computer right now. At least I could waste some time surfing the web. I gave up trying to occupy myself and closed my eyes while I waited for the breakfast tray. At least that would give me something to do. I heard a strange melody. It was coming from my purse. Ooh, my phone.

I snatched it up and a picture of Carter was staring back at me. I wasn't ready for this, but I answered the call anyway.

"Hello?" I answered hesitatingly.

"Good morning, beautiful. How are you feeling?" He sounded happy for seven thirty in the morning.

"Um, I'm feeling better. I still don't remember anything, though."

He didn't say anything for a few seconds. "Oh." He put a lot of disappointment into that one word.

"Cheryl said you were coming to pick me up today, is that still on?" I should give him an out in case he didn't want to deal with me or something.

"Of course I'll be there to get you. I just woke up and I wanted to see how you were this morning. I missed you last night."

"Oh, um, thanks." I didn't have anything else to say. Awkward.

"I'm going to take a shower and I'll be over there in about an hour. Can I bring you anything from home? I know Cheryl packed you some jeans to come home in, but do you want anything else?" I was barely listening after he mentioned the shower. He was going to be naked in my bathroom.

"No." Suddenly I remembered my baby. "How is Lucy doing?" Poor darling was surely feeling abandoned.

"She's fine, she misses you though. She had to make do and snuggle up with me last night." My dog was sleeping with Carter? What the hell? Oh, right. He was *in my bed*. Too much to think about.

I sat there in silence.

"Well, if you don't need anything I'll get

going so that I can get over there. I'll see you soon. I love you."

"Mmhmm." It was the only thing I could respond with. He disconnected and I sat there with the phone in my hand. I couldn't do this. I got a fresh wave of panicky thoughts. Cheryl's brother was coming to take me home. He lived in my house. What was I supposed to talk to him about? I knew he was artistic; there were drawings and weird sculptures he made all over Cheryl and Paulo's place. But I don't know squat about art so that topic wouldn't last long. Did he like romance novels? Cooking? Did we have anything in common?

I was snapped out of my musings by the rattle of the food cart. I had marked oatmeal for my breakfast since I usually don't eat before noon. At least I wouldn't be wasting some big meal. The same orderly from yesterday came in with my breakfast tray. Ah, coffee. He is a prince.

"Good morning. You want the oatmeal, right?"

"Right. Mostly I just need the coffee." I smiled as he placed the tray on the swivel table beside my bed and positioned it in front of me. "Thanks."

"No problem, see you at lunch," he said as he made his way out the door.

I hoped I wouldn't be here at lunchtime. I hoped I would be at home, reunited with Lucy and my memories.

I added the little sugar packet to my coffee. I usually take two, but there was only one on the tray so it would have to do, I needed the caffeine too much to quibble over sweetener. It was lukewarm, not optimal, but it was better than nothing. I sipped, trying to make it last since I didn't know if the hospital came around with refills. I lifted the dome over my breakfast. Not only was there a bowl of oatmeal, but also a piece of toast cut in triangles, a packet of margarine, yuck, and two little containers of jam, grape and strawberry. I put the lid back on and finished my coffee before I gulped down the tiny container of OJ. When I finished my beverages I pushed the table off to the side. I wanted to get dressed into real clothes, but I wasn't sure what the doctor would need from me, so I stayed in my pajamas and waited.

What seemed like an hour later, but was probably only a few minutes, Dr. Turner, my neurologist, came in.

"Justine, how are you feeling this morning?"

"I still don't remember. How long am I going to be like this?" I felt suddenly frantic. I had really believed I would wake up well and healed.

"I don't know. Every case is different. You might remember in an hour or it might take a few days. Perhaps once the swelling goes down. I can't really give you an exact time because it all depends on your body." He took out a penlight and shined it in my eye. It didn't hurt like it had when Robert had done it in the emergency room. That was progress in my book.

"Well, your pupils look fine, and none of your tests showed anything abnormal. I think once the inflammation goes down you'll be right as rain. I'm going to go get your release papers ready. Do you have someone coming to get you?"

"Yes, he'll be here in a little while."

"I'm going to want to see you again in a few days, but I'll put that in your instructions." He jotted down something and looked over at me seriously. "If you experience any dizziness or confusion, call my office."

"Okay. Thank you, doctor."

"I'll see you in a few days." The doctor left and I felt deflated. That was it? I wasn't well yet. I still had amnesia.

I sat there for a few minutes. There wasn't anywhere to go. Carter wasn't here yet, but I didn't want to be in night clothes when he arrived, so I got up and went over to the duffle bag. Ah, the jeans looked familiar. Finally. The shirt, not so much, it had some kind of metallic appliqué of birds on the front of it. Still, it was pretty cool. I took the jeans, tee shirt and some panties into the bathroom. Cheryl didn't pack me a bra, so I was going to be flying free, but at this point I didn't really care.

I felt a little bit more human after I changed. I decided to skip the shower, I'd be home soon and I would much rather take my time and have a bubble bath. I needed the stress relief. I stuffed my pajamas into the duffle bag and zipped it up, ready to go. I didn't put my shoes on since I was going to be lying on the bed, but I did put on the pink socks Cheryl had so kindly packed for me.

I was lounging on the hospital bed and staring at the ceiling when Carter walked in. Damn, he looked *good*. His dark wash jeans fit him to perfection and he was wearing a tee shirt that matched his gorgeous green eyes. It wasn't the first time I had noticed how good looking he was, but it was the first time I noticed while simultaneously acknowledging to myself that I have sex with him. Cue butterflies. It was the moment of truth. I was going to be going home. With him. To *our* house.

"Hey, you're looking better." He leaned down to give me a kiss, but at the last second I turned my head and his lips landed on my cheek. His smile evaporated and I felt like an ass.

He straightened back up and fixed the smile back on his face, but it didn't mask the hurt I could still see in his eyes. "Are you ready to blow this joint?"

"Yeah, let me get my shoes on."

I sat up and swung my legs off of the bed, but before I could get up to get my shoes Carter had already gone to the cupboard and gotten them for me. He handed them to me and gathered up the rest of the things in there, setting them next to my duffle bag. I slipped my shoes on and stood up. I was as ready as I was ever going to be.

"Let's go," I said with as much enthusiasm as I could muster.

Carter picked up my belongings and thrust a hoodie at me. "It's actually chilly this morning; you'd better put this on." I pulled it on as we walked down the hall. A small part of me was afraid to leave the relative safety of the hospital because, once at home, I was on my own. With Carter.

Chapter Five

We went out to the parking garage and Carter pushed the remote he had pulled out of his jacket pocket. We walked up to the same black truck I remembered from the other night. He walked around and opened the passenger door while I stood behind the vehicle like an idiot. Did I mention that being alone around a good looking man turned me into a stooge?

I managed to make my way to the door and tucked myself into the seat. Carter closed the door and walked around to his side but he stood there without opening it. I buckled my seatbelt and waited for him to get in. He didn't. I leaned over the center console and looked out the window. He was standing there with his eyes closed. Of course, a second later he opened them and looked directly at me. I couldn't breathe and I couldn't look away. We stayed there, still, and finally he grabbed the handle and opened the door.

He didn't say anything as he strapped in and started the truck. He didn't say anything as we left the hospital grounds and turned onto the street. He drove in silence until we got to my house.

Normally I wouldn't have minded this as it keeps me from having to make conversation. Right now, however, it was pissing me off. I didn't know why I was so angry, but each block of quiet ratcheted up my fury. By the time we pulled into my driveway I was ready to snap. Carter turned off the engine and sat in the seat looking forward.

"So, this is kind of weird, huh?" He turned his head to look at me.

"So you feel like talking to me now?" I reached down to the floor to grab my purse.

"Did I do something to upset you?" he asked as if he didn't know.

"Well, you ignored me for the entire car ride, which, *maybe*, has something to do with it." I reached for the door handle but Carter put his hand over mine and stopped me from pulling it.

"Is rage a side effect of a concussion? Wait. I'm sorry. I just didn't know what to say. You still don't remember me, not the right way. You turned your head when I kissed you. I don't know how I'm supposed to act around you. This is hard for me too, Justine." Carter's voice sounded ragged. But that wasn't enough to make me simmer down.

"You don't know what hard is. I don't have any idea who I am anymore. I don't know what I do. I sure don't know how I'm with you." After I said it, my anger fizzled out at the look on his face. I wasn't trying to be mean to him, I was just saying what I felt, but I realized that the last part didn't come out quite like I had intended.

He pulled his hand back and I opened the door. I wasn't in the mood to apologize to him, I had been through enough. So, even though I knew I had hurt his feelings, I got out and walked up the sidewalk.

Carter got out and beat me to the door. He unlocked it and stood aside to let me pass. I stopped several feet inside the doorway. My living room was wrong. There was a huge TV on one wall and long black table against the other. I took a few more steps and noticed other things that were different. There were several small metal statues on the built-in shelves that I recognized as his work and there were pictures in different styled chunky frames. Pictures of me, of Carter, of Cheryl and Paulo. There was no clutter. There were no magazines or cookbooks lying on the coffee table. It looked really nice, actually.

I turned to Carter. He was looking at me, staring really, but not in the same hopeful way as before. His face was blank. My stomach started to hurt. I'd obviously made him angry.

"It's different. I don't remember decorating it like this."

"I live here. What you don't recognize probably belongs to me." His tone was friendly but eyes weren't. I suddenly wanted the other Carter back, the overly familiar one that called me earlier.

I nodded and walked into the kitchen. Luckily, everything seemed to be in order there. My cookbooks were lined up on shelves beneath the island. All my countertop appliances were in their places and there were no extraneous items lying around. The only thing I noticed were some pieces of paper stuck to the refrigerator with magnets. I walked over and noted that they were recipes, written in my own handwriting with items scratched out and jotted down in the margins. I stared at them, not recognizing them, but intrigued.

"Those are the recipes you're working on right now." I wasn't aware that Carter followed me. "You've tried that Mexican gazpacho four times. I think it tastes great but you keep saying you can get it better." He walked over to the cabinet and pulled out a glass. "Are you thirsty?"

Suddenly I was parched. I nodded and he reached up for another glass.

"Iced tea?" I nodded again. It was surreal, Carter was playing host in my house. He pulled out a jug of sweet tea as I stood there. I had hoped coming home would restore my memory. It didn't, obviously, so I didn't really know where to go from here. I pulled out a stool and sat down at the island. Carter set my drink down and I wrapped my hands around it. Now what?

I knew it was time to ask Carter some important questions. Questions only he would be able to answer.

"What am I blocking out? What happened that's so terrible my mind won't let me remember?"

He looked at me, shocked, but after a moment he shook his head. "I don't know of anything terrible. You're happy. We're happy. I can't imagine what would make you forget your life. Us."

I sat there, holding my glass of tea and wishing I had some brilliant conversational skills that I could pull out now. I started to get a little nervous. I had just gotten home and I was already out of things to say and do. I couldn't work because I don't really know what it is I do. I've read blogs of course, but I've never set one up or written any. My cookbook sounded cool, but I don't know what's already in it or where to begin. There were so many things I had no knowledge of that it was overwhelming. I decided to start with something simple.

"Can I see my website? I don't even remember what it's called."

"It's Just Add Heat." He typed in the address into his phone and handed it to me.

I couldn't believe how good it looked. Professional. "Wow," I said as I scrolled down through the posts. "This looks great, when did I learn to do this?"

"You didn't. I designed the site. You told me what you wanted though." I scrolled lower, skimming the text on different posts.

"I'm pretty funny," I remarked with a smile. Holy moly, some of my posts had *hundreds* of comments. I kept going, clicking through some of the links and I saw a picture of myself. *I looked great!* Sexy, actually. Could that really be me? With the makeup and tame hair I looked like myself but way better. Being a chef and spending most of my time in a hot kitchen, makeup was simply something that I wore on a date, and my hair lived in a bun.

"That's a great picture, isn't it?" Carter was leaning over and looking at the screen. "Cheryl considers it her masterpiece."

"Yeah well, that's obvious. I didn't know I could look so good." I was wearing bright red lipstick and heavy eyeliner that made me look like I was made up for a red carpet appearance, and that's not to mention the way the top I was wearing gave me some *extreme* cleavage.

"I think you look beautiful all of the time. You don't need makeup to enhance your loveliness." He said it quietly.

I cringed. "I wasn't fishing for compliments, I know how I look."

"No Justine, I don't think you do." He lifted his hand up and pushed back a bit of hair that had escaped the scrunchie. His movement was tender, but it sent an electric shock through me.

I couldn't move, my eyes were locked with his and my breathing was shallow. I wanted to lean into his hand so I forced myself to blink, to break eye contact, and when I did he dropped his hand. I instantly felt the loss. It was so confusing. I didn't want him to touch me, I needed time, but at the same time it felt good.

Just then I heard a bark from outside the kitchen door. *Lucy*. My baby.

I jumped up and set the phone down as she launched herself through the doggy door. She barreled in with all her might and I scooped her up. "I missed you, girl. Have you been a good girl?" I asked, even though I knew she was. She was the best dog *ever*. Of course she didn't answer me, but she licked my face and moaned in her high pitched happy-dog way. At least this hadn't changed.

"She missed you, I did too. We didn't know what to do with ourselves last night." He reached over and rubbed Lucy's head. The fact that I was still holding her made the act more intimate. To me anyway. She leaned into his hand the way I had wanted to a minute earlier. Lucky dog. But, apparently I only had myself to blame. He was doling out the affection and I was cowering like a Victorian maiden.

I set Lucy down with a kiss and picked up my tea. I took a big gulp and set the glass down a little too hard. The whack of the glass hitting the countertop made me jump. I looked guiltily at Carter, but he wasn't looking at me. He wasn't looking at anything. I guess my continued lack of responses to his conversation was starting to take its toll. Again. My fault.

"Do you know what time Cheryl is coming by?" I asked as casually as I could. At least Cheryl being here would take some of the pressure off. I just wasn't able to relax around Carter while we were alone like this. It's not my fault.

"She said it would be sometime after one. She was staying until she was sure the caterers finished their job."

I looked at the clock. At least three more hours. How was I going to entertain him for three hours? I wracked my brain. There was that big TV out in the living room, maybe we could watch a movie, but that seemed lame. I don't even know what movies are out right now. I needed to work on getting my memory back. I needed to look at the rest of the house, to check for changes which might nudge my subconscious into action.

"I think I need to take a bath." That sounded stupid. It was ten a.m. and I just came home from the hospital. There was probably something else I should be doing, but I didn't know what.

"I'll go get your stuff from the car. You can get settled." I nodded again, and went down the hall to the bathroom. I flipped on the light and braced myself for changes but I was happily surprised, it looked pretty much the same except for the blue towels hanging on the rack. My towels were yellow. I surveyed the vanity with a critical eye. It was spotless and gleaming. Much cleaner than it usually looked. There was also men's cologne sitting on the left side of the counter. I picked it up and sniffed it. It smelled good, like Carter. I heard the front door open and I quickly put it down, unwilling to be caught in the act.

He appeared at the open door seconds later. "Do you want this in here?"

I nodded. "It's got my toothbrush and stuff." He handed me the bag and stood there. He was probably waiting for me to thank him for getting this. "Thanks Carter," I stammered, I had to get over this behavior.

"No problem, do you need anything else? Does your head feel okay?"

"I barely feel it. I'm just going to relax for a while. Thanks, for everything."

He gave a brief nod and stepped out of the bathroom. I shut the door behind him and turned to the tub. My favorite bath crystals were still in the jar on the shelf. I turned on the tap and poured some into the water. It started foaming up immediately and the smell of jasmine wafted up. I poured a little more in for good measure. I really needed this.

Once I stripped off my clothes I hurried back over to the door to make sure it was locked. It was and I felt a little foolish. It wasn't like he was going to come in here and try to catch me naked in the bath was it? Unless that's the kind of stuff he likes to do. I got goosebumps. Maybe he was kind of a perv that way, I don't know. I stepped in and hissed as the water enveloped my foot and calf. It was a little hotter than I usually liked, but perhaps that's just what I needed. I slowly lowered myself in the rest of the way, leaned back and closed my eyes. I felt my muscles slacken and I let out a deep breath. A second later I jolted upright as I heard a pounding on the door.

"Juss, are you okay in there?" I sat up and covered my breasts instinctively.

"Yeah, I'm fine I'm just going to lie here a while."

"You've been in there for over an hour, babe." *An hour?* I had just sat down. I then noticed the water was barely tepid. It had been scorching hot just a moment ago. Crap, am I passing out now, too?

"I'm getting out in a second. Thanks, I didn't realize how long I'd been in here."

"Okay, call me if you need anything."

"Okay." I waited until I heard him walk away before standing up and grabbing a towel off of the rack. I wrapped it around myself and stepped out and onto the rug as I looked at myself in the big mirror over the vanity. I still had the bruise on my cheek, of course, but my eyes seemed clearer than they had at the hospital. I started drying myself off and caught a glimpse of something on my back. There was a drawing of a flower on my shoulder. I turned in towards the mirror and looked closer. It was a tattoo.

"Oh my god!" I must have been out of my mind or drunk or something. I rubbed at it, but it didn't budge.

"What's wrong? What happened?" Carter's voice carried through the door a second later. What was he doing, skulking around in the hallway?

"I've got a tattoo," I told him with outrage.

"I know. I was there when you got it. I think it looks nice."

"I've never wanted a tattoo. What made me get this?" Perhaps it had been a dare; I never could pass up a dare.

"You got it after you quit the restaurant. It was your symbol of a new beginning. That's why the bud is still opening. You thought about it a long time before I drew it for you." I stood there, thinking about that for a moment. I turned more fully to look at the design. It *was* nice. Beautiful really, now that the shock was starting to wear off.

I suddenly remembered I was standing there in a towel and that I hadn't brought any clothes in with me. I searched through my bag but everything in there was dirty. Sanity returned and I opened up the cupboard where my robe was hanging. Thankfully, I still kept it there.

"Are you okay?" In my nakedness panic, I had forgotten that I hadn't said anything in response to him. Again.

"Yeah, I was just trying to get dressed. I'll be right out." I hurriedly pulled on my robe. I knew it was mine because it was silky and had flowers on it, but it wasn't the same one I remembered from a couple of days ago. Again, I was just rolling with the punches. It was like staying in someone else's house when you weren't planning on it and having to borrow their things. It felt foreign. I tied it around my waist and opened the door. Carter was still standing there, looking concerned, so I just gave him a weak smile and rushed past him to go to my bedroom.

I opened the closet and stopped dead. It was stuffed. All my clothes were pushed to one side and the other side was taken up by men's clothing. Stacks of jeans were on the shelves, and shoes were lined up along the entire floor area. My heart thumped hard against my breastbone. Everywhere I turned I was faced with the knowledge that I shared my life with Carter. My mind just refused to accept it.

Chapter Six

I grabbed a pair of black yoga pants off the shelf and snatched a red tee shirt before walking over to my dresser to grab a fresh pair of panties, only to encounter stacks of folded boxer briefs in various colors. I reached down to touch them but jerked my hand back at the last second. That was just wrong. Clearly *I* am the pervert. Who runs their fingers over someone's underwear?

I opened the drawer that used to be for my night wear. Bingo. Panties were staring back at me this time. I grabbed the first pair I saw and put them on, threw off the robe, and pulled on my clothes. Dressed, I didn't feel that I was as vulnerable. Not that I thought Carter was going to take advantage of me, but it made me feel better.

I walked back to the bathroom and Carter was no longer standing in the hallway. Good. I opened the cabinet that had all of my beauty essentials, basically brushes and hair ties, and pulled out a brush with soft bristles. I still hadn't detangled my hair, and I could tell that getting all the knots out was going to hurt and I didn't want to press my luck with the lump on my head. I pulled my hair out of the scrunchie and started gently working the brush through it, not an easy task in its greasy state. I really needed to wash it, but I was going to have to wait on that.

When I had gotten my hair as nice as it was going to get, I brushed my teeth and braced myself to go back out to the living room. When was I going to stop having to brace myself to do something? This had been the most stressful twenty four hours of my life. I was feeling drained mentally and physically.

All I wanted was to flop down on the couch, but I noticed Carter sitting there with his head thrown back, asleep with Lucy curled up next to him. I took the chance to observe him covertly. He was beautiful—I'd always thought so. When I first met him he was a bit gangly, but even then I could tell he was going to be a good looking man. Granted, he was only fourteen at the time, but he already looked like a model for some kind of perfume company. You know the kind of ads they shoot in black and white? Anyway, now he looked like every woman's fantasy. His body had filled out and his face had become more angular. His mouth, oh his mouth was gorgeous. It always looked like it was on the verge of smiling.

I found myself staring at his mouth. I could almost imagine it kissing my lips and enveloping my nipple. I imagined meeting his eyes as he looked up at me from between my legs. *What the hell?* I shivered, not knowing for sure if I was imagining the image or remembering.

I made my way closer to the couch and Lucy looked up at me and thumped her tail. It made Carter open his eyes so I guess he wasn't sleeping after all. I could feel the blush spreading over my face as I was caught staring at him.

"I'm a little hungry, you?" I asked him as nonchalantly as possible. I needed to get into the kitchen and cook something; sometimes it was the only thing that soothed my mind.

"I could eat. I haven't really been that hungry since your accident. Do you want me to call something in?"

"No, I feel like cooking. I'll go see what's in the fridge." I walked past him into the kitchen to peruse the offerings in the refrigerator. Hmm, I had plenty of vegetables and cheeses, but I was in the mood for Mexican food, maybe tomatilla enchiladas. It was one of my favorites, and it took a while to make, thereby killing two birds with one stone. I checked my supplies. The way my luck was running I wouldn't even have tortillas. Score! I still kept my pantry stocked with all the essentials. I picked up everything I needed and set it all down on the counter, grabbing the pans that I would use off of the pot rack over the island. For the first time since yesterday I felt a sense of normalcy. My whole body started to relax as I began chopping onions and garlic and heating up the cookware. I had been at it for a while when I heard Carter come up behind me.

"Do you want any help?" My body shivered as I recalled my thoughts of just a bit ago.

The question made me pause. I enjoyed cooking by myself, but I didn't want to be rude to Carter. "You could grate the cheese," I told him as I motioned to the fridge. "I need the Monterey Jack, oh and get out the sour cream as well." I slipped into chef mode as I directed him to do my bidding. He opened the door and I heard the drawers sliding open as he gathered the ingredients. He looked over at me where I stood peeling the paper from the tomatillas.

"Mmm. Green enchiladas?"

"Yep. I felt like Mexican." He set the items down and opened the cabinet in front of him, pulling out the yellow bowl I always used for mixing up the creamy sauce I poured on the enchiladas. "How did you know that I needed that bowl?" I asked him curiously.

"You always use this bowl. Actually, *I* always use this bowl because it's always *my* job to mix up the sauce."

I stared at him for a moment. Just how many times have we stood here making this dish together? Obviously he had done this enough times to recognize the dish by the ingredients. No one ever helped me cook in my home kitchen. This is where I come to relax. I didn't mind Cheryl so much, she just sat on a stool at the island and talked to me, but to have Carter be so familiar and me not actually minding that much was peculiar.

"Uh, then I guess you know what to do," I said lamely. He reached over to grab wooden spoon from the container in front of me and his proximity sent my senses on alert. He smelled amazing. The combination of his cologne and his manliness, mixed with the smells of the kitchen were like a trinity of awesomeness.

He took the grater out of the drawer and started on the cheese, and I couldn't help but notice the muscles in his forearm. They were taut and well defined, but not bulging like some weight lifter.

Mmm. I pulled myself out of my momentary daze and got back to work on my food.

Before I knew it, I was popping the pan of enchiladas into the oven. Carter and I had worked mostly in silence, but it wasn't awkward. It would have been harder for me to try and make conversation instead of giving myself a mental break and concentrating on my dish.

While it baked I started cleaning up the huge mess that always accompanied this recipe, and that's when it happened. I was standing at the sink and rinsing out a bowl when I turned to pick up the dish cloth from the counter and found myself chest to chest with Carter. I wasn't wearing a bra so as soon as my nipples scraped against him they stood to attention. I don't know what made me do it, but I pressed my face into his chest and sniffed his shirt. It smelled so good that I leaned in closer, until my forehead was up against him. He let out a quiet moan and I jerked my head back.

"I'm sorry," I gasped, appalled at myself. My blush of earlier had nothing on my flaming cheeks now. I busied myself with the bowl again and waited for him to step away, but he didn't. I scooted over to the side, just enough to break contact with him. I had to get myself under control. What the heck did I just do? Did I actually *sniff* him? Oh god, what am I doing? He's too young for me. I'm like some cougar. Well, no, I'm not that much older than him, maybe more like a bob cat.

What had possessed me? I stood there in acute embarrassment until he reached forward and touched my arm. "I like it when you smell me. You do it a lot. It's one of your things."

One of my things? Do I now go around sniffing on people? What kind of freak had I become? I must have looked horrified because he stepped closer. "I love it, actually." He leaned down to me as I stood there like I was hypnotized. His lips were on mine in the next second and I felt an electric jolt go from my lips to my chest to my belly button. I didn't even think as I opened my mouth to him. He put his hand on the back of my head and held me close. I was lost in sensation until I dropped the metal bowl I still had clutched in my hand, and it clattered into the sink making me jump and break the kiss.

I shook my head to clear my thoughts. That felt good. It felt like a first kiss, with my stomach tingling, but it also felt comfortable. I realized I was holding my breath, so I dragged in some air. Wow, he's a good kisser. I needed to step back and look at this situation. For all intents and purposes, we hadn't even gone on a date yet. It was as if someone you kind of know and are talking with starts kissing you out of the blue. You're surprised, even taken aback, but in the back of your mind you're thinking "Hmm. I wondered what kissing him would be like." If it's someone good looking you might even take the thought further and imagine sex. Or maybe that's just me.

Anyway, I did the only sensible thing I could do in this situation—I dashed out of the kitchen. I know it was cowardly, but I didn't care. I just had to get out of there, taking refuge in my bedroom. I flopped down on the bed and tried to bring my breathing back to normal. It didn't work. Even here I was confronted with Carter.

There was a picture of the two of us on the night

stand, next to the old fashioned alarm clock. A button down shirt was tossed over the chair in the corner. The comforter on the bed was also not as I remembered. It was brown like my old one, but it was a lot darker and puffier. I closed my eyes and tried to get my bearings. Okay, so kissing Carter wasn't such a bad thing. What was I freaking out about? Sure, it was all new, but it wasn't *bad*. I could, in some alternate reality, see myself possibly becoming involved with him. Unfortunately, I was in *this* reality. The reality where I was a thirty year old woman with amnesia and Carter was my best friend's little brother. Well, younger anyway, he was definitely larger than Cheryl.

So I sat there feeling sorry for myself. I felt sorry about not working at the restaurant, I felt sorry for hurting Carter's feelings, but mostly I felt sorry about having no memory of the past two years. I couldn't remember the good times or the bad. I looked over at the clock. Shit, the enchiladas would be ruined. I jumped up and hurried into the kitchen only to be met with a pan of perfectly cooked enchiladas sitting on the stovetop. I skidded to a stop. The kitchen was spotless. Carter had scrubbed the pans, done the dishes, and put everything away. So, apparently he was some perfect guy, he cooks, he cleans, he's helpful, and most importantly, he's hot. Well, maybe not most importantly, but it's pretty darn important to me. So yeah, he looked good on paper, but if everything's so awesome, why couldn't I remember living with him? It all came back to that.

I went to the pantry; I was craving some Mexican rice to eat with the enchiladas. I grabbed a jar of my favorite salsa to pour in and pulled down a pot. I hadn't even opened the bag of rice before Carter was back in the kitchen.

"Thanks for cleaning up and for saving lunch."

He nodded. "No problem. I'm sorry about earlier. I promised myself that I would give you time, but you leaned into me and I … well, I'm sorry." He remained standing where he was so I went back to measuring out my rice. I wanted to pretend everything was normal, but inside I was in turmoil. When were things going to be right?

I put the lid on the pot and turned on the burner. He didn't move. I guess he was waiting for me to say something else, but I had nothing. I looked at the clock on the stove, twelve thirty. Cheryl would be here soon. That would take some of the pressure off, I hoped.

"I hope Cheryl is hungry."

"She is. She called me while you were resting." I appreciated the fact that he said resting as opposed to hiding. "She wanted to know how you were doing and to ask if you wanted her to come alone or to bring Paulo. He's worried about you too. I told her you'd let her know when you got up."

"Oh, of course she should bring Paulo. I don't know why I didn't think of it myself. I'll call her now." I went over to the table and dug my phone out of my purse. She picked up on the first ring.

"Justine?" she questioned happily.

"Hey Cheryl. Carter just told me you called. Of course bring Paulo; I'd love to see him. I made tomatilla enchiladas, I know he loves them."

"Have you remembered anything?" she asked hesitantly. I wasn't sure what the whole Carter's mouth thing was earlier, so I just told her no.

"Well, I'll be leaving here in about five minutes. I'm just making sure everything is in order before I go. We'll be there in about half an hour, okay?"

"That sounds great. See you soon." I disconnected the call and felt better. Spending time with Cheryl and Paulo was something normal. I could remember that. Maybe everything would be okay after all.

"Can I help you with anything?" For a moment I had forgotten Carter was standing behind me.

"I'm good, thanks. Cheryl and Paulo will be here in about half an hour." I didn't know what else to say. We obviously needed to talk. We had a lot of things to discuss, not the least of which was where he would be staying tonight, but now was not the time, I was about to have lunch with my friends.

I set the timer for the rice before I made my way back to the living room. Lucy was still on the couch, rolled up in a little ball so I sat down beside her and stroked her soft fur. She shifted under my hand and I felt a bit better.

I looked over at the bookshelves again. I had just given them a cursory glance when I got home, but now I took the time to notice the changes. Small metal figures were placed in random areas, interspersed with books. I got up to look more closely. They were beautiful. Some were shaped like people, alone and entwined. One looked like it was made of liquid. I had to put my hand out and touch it, almost surprised when I encountered a solid object. I knew they belonged to Carter, were made by him, even though I had no recollection of them. I had seen other, similar pieces in Cheryl's parents' house. They added a nice touch to my living room. I had never been much into decoration, in fact, my home was pretty minimalist. Not utilitarian, just simple. That's the way I had always liked things. Simple.

I moved along the wall and came to what I thought was a lamp. It wasn't, well, maybe it was, but the base was a large glass bowl, and inside were two angel fish, a white and yellow one and a black and blue one. I had never felt the need to own fish. They didn't give you love, not like a dog or even a cat. They just stayed in their bowl, swimming in circles. I touched the glass and the black one zipped to where my finger was. It was like it was trying to say "Hi". A second later it swam off and I remembered that fish only have a three second memory. I could relate.

I wanted to scream. Perhaps that would loosen something in my mind. Without a second thought I opened my mouth and screamed at the top of my lungs. It felt liberating until Carter flew into the room with a look of terror on his face.

"What happened?" He took hold of me and gathered me to him as he looked around.

"Nothing," I responded, ashamed of myself for giving in to such a childish desire. "I was just frustrated." He released me slowly, but not before I felt his heart pounding. I felt bad for frightening him and for forgetting I wasn't alone. Lucy was standing up on the couch looking around in confusion and it made me feel even worse.

"You scared the shit out of me, Justine." He ran a hand through his already disheveled looking hair.

"Sorry," I whispered. I seemed to be feeling that a lot today. We stood there for what seemed like a long time, but really was only a few seconds. I was happy to hear the timer on the stove start beeping.

"I need to get that." I made my way around him, leaving him standing beside the couch. He looked lost, too. At least it wasn't just me feeling this way. I turned off the burner and looked around. On closer inspection I could see that there were some changes in here as well. There were orange and brown woven placemats on the table and some kind of ceramic napkin rings holding real napkins. I was used to paper napkins, it was less of a bother and I'm a busy woman. But, the look worked, it was warm and inviting. I approved.

The doorbell chimes jolted me out of my thoughts. Yay! Cheryl was here and I don't think I'd ever been happier to see her.

Chapter Seven

My smile was one of happiness as well as relief. I could relax, if only for a little while. I made my way out to the living room as Carter was opening the door. My smile got wider as I saw Paulo's dark head behind Cheryl.

"Cheryl, Paulo, I'm so glad you're here." They couldn't possibly know how glad I was right then. I was still feeling foolish about screaming a minute ago. Just thinking about that made me cringe. Great, now I was blushing, too. I met them in the middle of the room as Carter took their jackets. Just like he lived here. I reached out and gave Cheryl a hug and then Paulo pulled me in for another.

"You doing okay, honey?" he asked me in his Portuguese accent. Cheryl had met Paulo our senior year while he was here on a student visa. They fell in love and he never went back.

"I'm good. A little freaked out, though." I shrugged as I stepped back and motioned them to come in farther. "Are you hungry? I just finished the rice. We can eat anytime."

"I can smell my favorite enchiladas, Justine. You

know I'm ready." Paulo put me at ease immediately. I was glad he had come along and I was also glad I had made the enchiladas. Suddenly I felt that maybe everything *was* going to be okay. I took a deep breath as Carter turned back from the coat closet and sent me a smile. A real one. Not one like he's just humoring the weirdo who screams out loud for no reason. I felt warm inside.

"Let's eat, I haven't had anything since lunch yesterday," Carter said this as we walked into the kitchen, and I felt a tug on my heart. Even I had eaten and I was the one who was in the hospital.

We all busied ourselves with various tasks. Cheryl got drinks for everyone while Carter and Paulo set the table. Once everyone was seated we started serving ourselves. I was glad they were here. It just felt like family. Not like my family, which consisted of only Gloria since my father had ditched her before I was born, but a close, normal family that actually liked to be around each other. The family I had always craved.

"So Justine, any breakthroughs since you've been home?" Paulo asked.

"Uh no, nothing." I was embarrassed to admit to no improvement.

"She's only been home for a few hours, give her a break." Carter was speaking to Paulo but looking at me. I hurriedly looked back down at my plate and scooped up some rice, shoving it into my mouth so quickly that some of the grains went down my throat. I started coughing and grabbed for my water, gulping it down. I looked up and everyone was staring at me.

"Sorry, it went down the wrong way," I croaked out. Why couldn't I just be smooth for once? I slowly brought a bite of enchilada to my mouth and daintily started to chew. Everybody else went back to eating so I turned to Cheryl.

"How was the christening?"

"Fine. The parents went all out on this thing. There were almost as many guests as my wedding. I hope they call me to plan his first birthday party." The mention of her wedding made me feel bad again. I didn't know how many people came to her wedding. That was something a best friend should know.

"How are you coming with the cookbook?" Paulo asked between bites.

"I don't know," I said stupidly. I looked at Carter and waited for him to answer. He was probably the only one of us that knew.

"It's coming along. She's pretty much figured out what she's putting in there. We were just talking about if she was going to make the food for the pictures or hire a food stylist."

Hire a food stylist for my own book? I don't *think* so. Then again, I didn't even know what recipes were in there so maybe I shouldn't jump to conclusions.

"Either way, my pictures will make them fabulous." Paulo was an excellent photographer whose work was often featured in magazines, even so, Cheryl groaned at his statement. "What?" Paulo's confidence was something that I was familiar with and that made me happy. Things felt kind of normal in a weird "time moved forward two years overnight" way.

Lunch progressed without further incident and before I realized it most of the afternoon had gone by in idle chatter about nothing in particular. It's not like I would be up-to-date on anything recent. That would have been cool on a regular day, but I kept waiting for something to clue me in to the present. Nothing happened and by four Cheryl and Paulo were getting ready to go home. I couldn't let Cheryl leave without having an important talk.

"Cheryl, can I talk to you for a second?" I motioned toward my bedroom. "In my room."

"Sure." She followed me and shut the door. "What's wrong?"

"Everything's wrong, but I just needed to talk to you about Carter. What am I supposed to do?" I sat down on the bed.

"Do about what?" She looked confused.

"Well, I mean, I don't know where he's going to sleep or anything. What am I supposed to do with him tonight? I've never spent this much time alone with him before. I'm running out of things to talk about."

She looked at me and didn't say anything for a beat. "I don't know what to say to you about this, you *love* being around him. You guys spend all your time together. You're always laughing at some inside joke or whispering between yourselves. I would feel left out if I didn't have Paulo."

I took a moment to absorb that. We were one of *those* couples. I couldn't get my mind around it. I had *never* been like that in any relationship, not even in high school. It seemed like I was a completely different person.

"But what am I supposed to do with him *tonight*?" It didn't appear that Cheryl was getting the import of what I was saying.

"Have him sleep on the couch. It's okay, he won't

be mad at you, he'll understand. Don't get yourself worked up over it." She rubbed my upper arm. "Do you want us to stay a while longer?"

"No, that's okay. I'll be okay." I said this more for myself than for her.

We sat there for a few more seconds and then she stood up and walked back out to the living room. The guys were sitting on the couch playing with Lucy who was burning around the living room in tight circles with her toy gripped in her teeth. Carter looked up when we came in but didn't say anything. Paulo stood up and handed Cheryl her jacket.

We hugged goodbye and they were gone. It was just the two of us again. We hadn't cleaned the kitchen after lunch, just set the dishes on the counter, so I made my way to put everything in the dishwasher. Carter followed me and pulled out a clean dishrag as I started rinsing off the plates and utensils. I was nervous about being alone in the kitchen with him after what happened earlier, but the dishes had to get done and I couldn't avoid him forever.

He wet the rag and squeezed a bit of dish soap on it, and I thought he would be all anal and pre-wash the plates or something, but he walked over to the table and wiped it down instead. I put everything in the dishwasher and Carter put the leftovers into plastic containers. I noticed we were a good team as far as working in the kitchen. For some reason that made me extremely happy. We were done in only a few minutes and I was stressing about how to spend the rest of the evening, but Carter was ahead of me on that one, too.

"Want to watch a movie?" he asked as I turned on

the dishwasher.

"Um, sure." I was actually relieved. That would take up a couple of hours that I didn't have to make conversation. It was starting to feel awkward again.

"We can see what's on cable or we can go rent something if you'd rather."

I knew he was being polite, letting me make the choice, but I was painfully aware that I didn't know any of the movies from the past years, so anything on cable was likely to be new to me.

"Whatever's on is fine. I'd like to just veg out." That actually sounded like heaven right at this moment. I was still dressed in the yoga pants and tee shirt, so I didn't even need to change into more comfortable clothes. I grabbed a fresh glass since I had just put everything away and turned to Carter. "Would you like a drink?"

"Sure, I'll take a Coke." That sounded good to me too so I grabbed two cans and filled both glasses with ice. He took the cans from me and started for the living room. I trailed after him with a tingle in my stomach. We were going to watch a movie. Alone. I felt a little giddy. Foolish, I know, but I still have a pulse. Did I mention that Carter is *hot*?

We settled ourselves on opposite sides of the couch and Carter picked up the remote. He held it out to me, but I waved it off. This wasn't the twenty inch TV I was used to, it was a big flat screen behemoth. Even the remote looked too complicated. He turned it on and started flipping through the channels. I was only vaguely aware of what he was doing; I was too busy watching Carter's beautiful fingers work the remote.

"Is this okay?" His voice broke me out of my

reverie.

"Huh?" I jerked my eyes away from his hand and up to his face.

"*Anchorman*. It's pretty good. You like it."

"Sure. That sounds great." I actually remembered that movie, since it was several years old.

"It doesn't start for ten more minutes; do you maybe want to talk?"

He was looking serious. I hoped this wasn't going to be anything bad. "Okay. What do you want to talk about?"

"Do you remember anything at all, about us, I mean?" He looked into my eyes, so hopeful, but I couldn't lie.

"I'm sorry Carter, I don't. The last thing I remember is you being at Cheryl's house eating pizza and watching a movie. I was pissed off at John for canceling out on me on my night off and Cheryl told me to come over."

At the mention of John, Carter's face tightened. I didn't mean to upset him; I was just telling him my last memory of the two of us even being in the same room. Now he just looked dejected. I wanted to lean over and pat his arm or something, but I was too chicken to touch him. I wasn't sure I could control myself; I might sniff him again or something. Uh, my stupid face with its stupid blushes.

I turned my head forward. Maybe he wouldn't notice that I was a spazz.

"What's wrong? Why is your face all red?" Well, so much for him not noticing.

"I'm fine." Crap, Carter noticing my blush just made it worse. Now he would know it was something embarrassing, but there was no way I was going to tell him what I was thinking about.

"Do you want to know anything?" Boy did I. It was just that I suddenly felt shy and I didn't have the mental fortitude to start asking a bunch of personal questions that I wasn't ready to know the answers to just yet.

I shook my head and Carter sighed. What did he want from me? I just got home from the *hospital* for goodness sake. I couldn't deal with this emotional crap right now. How was I supposed to take it all in? I needed to deal with this in baby steps, and learning about a relationship that I have no recollection of is like some kind of giant moon step. I reached forward and grabbed my can of soda, popping the top and pouring it over my ice. It started foaming over the rim of the glass and onto the coffee table.

"Dang it!" What else was going to go wrong today? No, scratch that, I didn't need to invite trouble. I lifted my glass off of the table and started slurping the foam from the side. I didn't even notice Carter had gotten up to get a towel until he thrust it in front of me.

"Here." He handed me a paper towel and used another one to wipe off the table. .

"Thanks." Could I look more like an imbecile? How embarrassing.

"No problem," He didn't say anything else and took the paper towels back into the kitchen. He came back with two clean ones; I guess he wasn't sure I was going to be able to drink without further mishap.

Once he sat down again he picked up the remote and turned the volume on. I guess sharing time was over. He must have realized I couldn't be counted on for coherent conversation and decided watching previews for other movies was easier all around. That suited me just fine.

I made myself more comfortable and put my feet up on the coffee table. Hmm. My toes looked pretty nice. The polish wasn't even chipped. It looked like a fresh pedicure. Nice color. I tried to remember the last time I had gone to the nail place. It had been a while, and this looked like a professional job. Then again, why would I pay someone to do something I could take care of in five minutes? I must be getting better at it. I nodded and wiggled my toes. I did a dang good job.

The sounds of the movie starting made me stop admiring my feet. Carter turned off the lamp next to him and turned up the volume. I fixed my eyes on the screen, but it couldn't hold my attention. The last thing I remembered was Will Ferrell doing a cannonball.

Mmm, so warm. Wait, what? I opened my eyes to the bottom of Carter's chin.

"What are you doing?" Suddenly I was totally awake.

"I'm putting you to bed; you've had a long day." I looked outside the window—it was still light out.

"It's too early. I was just taking a nap. Put me down." He put me down on the bed, and I immediately stood back up. I looked at the clock. "It's only six thirty. I'm not ready for bed." I shook my head at him.

So here we were, in my bedroom. Everything was abruptly awkward.

"So um, you're sleeping on the couch, right?" I just blurted it out, so much for trying to finesse the situation.

He raised his eyebrows as if he hadn't thought of it at all. "Oh, yeah, that was the plan." Yeah right. I could tell by his face that I had caught him off guard with that.

I stifled a yawn. Maybe I *was* tired. I was planning on a shower so that I could wash my hair, but that could wait until tomorrow. Did I have to do anything tomorrow?

"What day is it?" I asked. It was strange to not know such a simple thing.

"Sunday." He was still standing there. Tomorrow was Monday. Usually I was off on Monday nights, it was the slowest, but I normally went in early in the day to check the stock and order what was needed. It took me a second to remember that I no longer go in on Mondays or any days for that matter.

"What do I do on Mondays? Do I have something I need to get done?"

"Not really, you've been spending most of your time on your book, you usually post something on Tuesdays, but if things are still...like this, I'll post that you're sick or something."

Oh. Well, surely Carter works on Mondays, but I couldn't remember what he told me he did. If so, tomorrow I could spend my time going through my things and trying to remember.

"What time do you go to work?" I asked as casually as possible.

"I already called my boss. I'm taking a few days off, just to make sure you're all good."

"Please don't take off on my account. I don't want to get you in trouble or anything." I was trying to get a little alone time because I really didn't know how I was going to get through another day like this one.

"It's fine. Mr. Webster told me to take as much time as I need until you're back to normal."

Nuts. Well, there was nothing to do in this situation but call it a night. Lucy had followed us in here and was already curled up on the bed. Bedtime was her favorite time of the day and I was leaning toward her way of thinking right now.

"I think I am a little sleepy. I'm just going to get ready for bed." I hoped he would take the hint and leave, but it wasn't happening.

I raised my eyebrows for emphasis when he didn't make any move to go.

"Oh. I guess I need to grab my stuff." He didn't hurry, but strolled across the room to the dresser and took out a pair of boxer briefs before walking to the closet to pull out a tee shirt and some sweat pants. "Call me if you need anything." He walked out of the room and I was left standing there, confused. That didn't go like I thought it would. He didn't even put up any resistance. I felt strangely deflated.

I flounced over to the dresser and opened drawers until I found my sleepwear. There were fewer boxers and more night shirts than I remembered, but I still chose a pair of shorts and a tee shirt. I didn't want to chance wearing something that Carter might take as an invitation. I pulled on my night clothes, but I wasn't really ready to sleep, so I went out to get a book off of the shelf in the living room.

When I walked past the bathroom door I heard the shower running. I felt my stomach tighten. This couldn't keep happening. I felt like I was *crushing* on him. Geez, what was I, twelve? I hurried down the hall and into the living room, seizing a book at random, but relieved to see it was a Nora Roberts title that I remembered. At least I could open it to any page and know where I was in the story. I went into the kitchen, grabbed a bottle of water out of the refrigerator, and made my way back to my room. Just as I came to the bathroom door it opened and I was suddenly staring directly at Carter's bare chest.

I stopped, blocked by the exquisiteness that was Carter's unclothed torso, and stood there, unspeaking, just long enough to appear creepy before I pulled myself together.

"Sorry." I scurried past him and back into the bedroom, closing the door and leaning up against it while I got my breath back under control. This rooming together thing was going to be tougher than I thought.

Chapter Eight

I pushed off from the door, set my water and book on the bedside table, and flopped down on the bed. There was something I was missing here. I struggled to come up with a good reason why I was so opposed to the idea of being with Carter. Really, the only major stumbling block was that he was Cheryl's brother, and that was always in that "no go" area of boyfriends. If there was a breakup, the friend always had to stick with blood. At least I assumed that was what happened; I didn't have any siblings that I could test this theory with.

Then there was the fact that he was younger than me. It was a little bit weird, just because I knew him when he was younger, but he definitely wasn't a kid anymore.

I sat up and puffed the pillows up behind me and settled back on the bed. I noticed that it was a little cool in the room, but the thermostat was out in the hallway and there was no way in the world I was going out there to adjust it tonight. I got up and pulled the comforter and sheet back and crawled in, snuggling down, and Lucy crawled under and pressed up against my legs like a little hot water bottle. Things felt normal. Well, besides the fact that there was a half-naked man somewhere out there in my house.

I snatched my water and chugged some down. I had better watch my liquid intake; I didn't want to have to go to the bathroom any time soon. I screwed the top back on and picked up my book, but I just couldn't concentrate on it. I read the same paragraph three times before I realized I hadn't absorbed a single word; I was too busy listening for sounds from outside the door. I looked around for something else to occupy my time but nothing jumped out at me.

I threw back the covers and stood up; there had to be something in here that would give me some window into my recent past. I opened the closet but there were only clothes. I went over to the other bedside table. Aha! There were some books stacked in the bottom space. I pulled one out a scrapbook of some kind. I don't do scrap booking, so I had already found something foreign to me. The first page was a big picture of Carter. He was obviously laughing and I could see his teeth. He has nice teeth. I had noticed that earlier.

I started paging through, seeing pictures of me and of Carter in various poses and activities. There was one of us on a roller coaster. I was screaming with my eyes shut but Carter had his hands up, again he was laughing. I felt a little tug in my chest. He and I had gone to an amusement park. I knew I was dorky like that, and I could never find anyone to do that kind of stuff with me, but apparently Carter didn't mind it so much. He looked happy in the photo. In fact, he was smiling in every picture I had come across so far. I realized that he hadn't been smiling much today and I could only assume it was my fault. Well, clearly it was my fault, but what was I supposed to do? I wasn't going to fake some grand love. Things were tough enough as it was.

I shut the book, more frustrated than before. I wished I had my laptop in here, at least then I could get online, but it was in the office. Oh my phone! I looked around before remembering that I had left it in the kitchen. Crud. What if I needed to make a call in the middle of the night? What if someone called me? I weighed the pros and cons of going out there. Really, the only con was that I would encounter Carter. That really wasn't a con so much as me being a chicken and I needed my phone.

I looked at the clock. *What?* It was only seven fifteen. The time was crawling at a snail's pace. There was no way I was going to be able to hole up in here for several more hours or until I got sleepy. I decided to be brave and sneak into the office, really, just the tiny room across the hall. I could get online and I wouldn't even have to venture out to the kitchen.

Lucy was still under the covers so I quietly went to the door and peeked out. The coast was clear; I could hear the TV, so I was especially glad that I had decided against getting my phone as I pushed open the door. Double crap! He was sitting at a drafting table that I had never seen before and he looked up at me. At least he had his shirt on now.

"Everything okay?" His pencil had stopped moving while he fixed his gaze on me. I felt self-conscious in my baggy faded tee shirt but that only lasted for a moment before my eyes were drawn from him to the walls.

Shelves now hugged every visible wall surface, but that's not what held my attention. The Star Wars dolls looking at me from every direction did that. I blinked to make sure I wasn't hallucinating but they were still there when I opened my eyes. What the *hell*? There were probably a hundred or more dolls still in packages gazing down at me. Everywhere I turned there was more Star Wars memorabilia. I'm talking space ships and light sabers.

"What is this?" I gestured around the room.

"Rebel Base." He smiled and looked over his shoulder.

The only thing that I could recognize was my desk, but even that looked different somehow. *Oh my god.* My mind went straight to those freaks that congregate at SciFi conventions. I had never been to his apartment so this new side of him took a moment to absorb. I threw him a glance over my shoulder and he was still beaming proudly. *Geek!*

"I was just going to get on the computer, but since you're busy I'll just go get my phone." I turned to go but he jumped up off of the stool before I could duck out.

"Wait. You can get on the computer, you won't be bothering me." He walked over the desk and turned on a computer with a massive screen.

"What happened to my other computer?"

"It's over there." He pointed to a shelf above a life sized R2D2 where a laptop was sitting.

"This is mine, but it's the main one we use." I walked over to the desk and sat down. I would have preferred to be alone, but now I was trapped inside a Star Wars fanboy's wet dream.

I decided to ignore the décor and focus on things

that I could possibly deal with. "Can you tell me how to get to my website? I'd like to look at it a little closer." He leaned over and typed in the address and it popped up quickly. It looked even better on this larger screen. "Thanks."

He sat back down on his stool and rolled it next to me. I was engrossed in no time. It was something that I would have loved reading if I stumbled across it. I clicked on a link to a cooking segment and my kitchen was suddenly filled the screen. This was the coolest thing *ever*. The camera zoomed in on me as I spoke about fiery béchamel sauce, and the right way to make it. I realized right away why my clips went viral; my on camera persona was a vamp. It was completely different from my day to day behavior, but it was entertaining.

I switched to a clip where I was making a watermelon Italian ice and I laughed at my off-color joke about my melons. My chest swelled. I was good, even though it looked like my dress was painted on. I guess it was really true that sex sells. I finished that clip and went to the next. I sounded so knowledgeable about spicy minestrone. Anyone could make it after watching this, and hey, if people wanted to see me talking dirty to food, who was I to deny them? I didn't realize how absorbed I was until I heard Carter speaking from next to me.

"You're great, aren't you? You should read the feedback on that episode. It was phenomenal." He sounded so proud of me. He was smiling as he watched the video. My stomach flipped over. His smile made him look so beautiful that for a second I couldn't breathe. I quickly turned my face back to the screen so that I didn't get caught staring at him again.

"It's awesome. I can't believe it's me." We fell back into silence but I was acutely aware of him right beside me. He still smelled fresh from the shower. I decided to breathe with my mouth; I couldn't chance any adverse reactions. That clip finished and I clicked open portabella stroganoff. Mmm. I was getting hungry now. Stroganoff sounded good.

"What's the matter?"

"Huh?"

"Why are you breathing so loudly?" Oh shoot, I forgot I was breathing through my mouth like some Neanderthal. I quickly took a breath through my nose.

"I guess I was just getting excited about the stroganoff." I tried to play off my panting but I didn't think he was buying it. I could feel him looking at me and my face started flaming. Again.

"Are you hungry? It's been hours since lunch." I was starving, but I wasn't going to admit it.

"I'm okay; I'll probably make a sandwich in a little while." My evil, treacherous stomach decided to growl right then.

"You stay here and relax; I'll make us some sandwiches." He was up and out the door before I could come up with an excuse for him not to. I felt I could finally relax with him and his aroma no longer next to me.

R2D2 was staring at me like he could read my mind so I clicked back to the blog page and started scanning the feedback from my readers. Well, I guess you could call them fans. Holy moly, I have fans! This was way cooler than someone sending compliments back to the kitchen through the server.

But I couldn't get a big head. I didn't really know how to do this. My future self had fans. Me, not so much. I was still skimming down the page when Carter came back in with Lucy on his heels. He handed a plate to me. Cheese sandwich, chips and a napkin.

"Thank you." I didn't want to start scarfing down the food right away but I was *really* hungry. I grabbed a chip, and the crunch was thunderous in the small room so I made sure my lips were completely sealed before I continued to chew. Carter didn't seem to mind. He sat down on the stool with his plate and started in on his food. Great, now I was self-conscious. I picked up my sandwich without looking at Carter and turned back to the computer. We ate in silence uninterrupted by any choking or spilling on my part. I considered that a success.

Lucy was begging at my knee so I pulled off a piece of cheese. She gobbled in down without chewing. I guess she gets it from me. When she saw I had no more to give her she went to beg from Carter. Little traitor. Carter gave her the last bit of his sandwich, so I stood up to take my plate back to the kitchen, eager to make my escape.

"Are you finished with that?" I held out my hand for his plate and he passed it to me.

"Thanks honey." Did he call me honey on purpose? Was I being too sensitive? I turned my head to him, waiting for him to say "sorry" or something but he didn't. It was like he was challenging me to call him on it. We had an eyeball duel for a few seconds before I broke off, admitting to myself I wasn't going to say anything. I fled the Star Wars museum and rinsed off the dishes half expecting Carter to follow me into the kitchen, but he never showed. The dishwasher had finished with the load so I emptied it, but still no Carter. I knew it was twisted to want him to follow me just so I could knock him back. Well, maybe not knock him back, just discourage him.

Maybe I was just perverse. He had been nothing but kind and supportive of me since the accident. It's true that I didn't remember being with him like *that*, but I would be lying to myself if I denied being curious. Sure, it now appeared he was a nerd thereby lessening his coolness, but that nerd could kiss.

There, I said it. The kiss earlier in the day had been awesome and no amount of blocking it out or pretending it never happened was going to change that. I wanted to kiss him again. Was it wrong to want to kiss him as *this* Justine as opposed to the one he's involved with? Because *this* Justine didn't have any qualms about seeing where this could go. That future Justine however was standing in my way. *I* wasn't who Carter wanted to kiss, that was future Justine.

God, it was just too much to handle. Had it only been since yesterday that my whole world had been turned upside down?

My phone started ringing in my purse so I pulled it out and looked at the face staring back at me. I didn't have a clue who it was. It said Elisa, but that didn't help me at all. I held it until it stopped ringing and went to voicemail. It hit me again that I didn't know what all I'd missed. She might be my new best friend, though I didn't think so. I thought about going and asking Carter, but for some reason I didn't want to do that, either. Something about her gave me a funny feeling that I didn't want to delve into too deeply so I just shoved the phone back in my bag and looked around the kitchen.

I tried to imagine myself standing at the island and making my cooking videos. I went over to the refrigerator to read my recipes again. A second later I pressed my head to the freezer door and burst into tears. Obviously, the pressure was getting to me. Why couldn't I remember? It wasn't fair! I had this supposedly perfect life and I couldn't even enjoy it. I didn't know how long I stood there crying before I felt arms coming around me.

"Juss," he whispered into my ear. He turned me around and pulled me close. I started crying harder. He stroked my hair and all I wanted was to be with him, it felt *right*.

I tipped my head up. "Kiss me, Carter." He hesitated for only a second before he brought his head down to mine. I felt his lips and suddenly I couldn't get enough of him. His lips, his tongue, and god, his smell. I brought my hands up to pull his head closer to mine while he backed us against the refrigerator. I sucked his bottom lip into my mouth and he groaned as I tasted his tongue and felt the heat of his mouth in mine.

I made a noise in the back of my throat and after a second he pulled back.

"Why are you stopping?" I panted out.

"This isn't right." He took my hands from the back of his head and placed them at my side.

I couldn't believe he was rejecting me. I felt like I had been punched in the stomach. "Are you kidding me?" I could barely say the words out loud.

"No, I'm so sorry Justine, but you're not ready for

this. I wish to god you were, but..."

"But nothing," I spat. "I can't believe you. You're in my face all day, but the minute I give you some encouragement you push me away." I shoved past him and ran back to my room but not before my tears started flowing again.

I had barely slammed the door behind me when it was thrust back open.

"Get out."

"No. Listen, I would never forgive myself if..."

"*Get out!*" I felt the need to yell it this time since he hadn't felt inclined to listen to me the first time.

"No," he yelled back. "Do you think I wanted to stop? Hell no. I *had* to. You're fragile right now. I won't take advantage of this situation. I fucking *love* you. If you don't know anything else right now, I want you to understand *that*."

I didn't want to cut him a break, but looking at his face I didn't have any choice. He was hurting. I was scared and confused but I didn't remember loving him, so I wasn't *hurting*.

I stood there breathing heavily with tears running down my face. He moved closer and pulled me back into his arms.

"I love you." He said the words gently this time and in that moment it was the only thing in the world that I knew for sure.

Chapter Nine

We stood there with Carter clutching me for several minutes. I couldn't move. It wasn't that he was holding me captive; it was that my legs refused to carry me away from him.

Finally, he loosened his hold and I took a step away from him. Hopefully, tonight my mind would reset and I would wake up tomorrow with everything in my world in its proper place.

"I'm going to go to bed now, Carter." He looked down at me and I knew he wanted to say something but he remained silent. "Goodnight," I told him after he made no move to leave.

"Goodnight, love." He pushed a piece of my hair behind my ear but made no move to kiss me again. *Hmph.* He walked over to the bed and pulled off a pillow before going to the chest sitting under the window and taking out a blanket. He didn't say anything else as he walked from the room, he didn't even look back at me.

Oh man, I had completely lost my mind. I flopped on the bed with Lucy and moaned. I couldn't believe that I demanded that he kiss me then yelled at him when he stopped. I grabbed my pillow and covered my head with it. I seek out ways to humiliate myself; it was the only explanation. Maybe I did have brain damage. They didn't say for sure that I didn't. Maybe the doctor would call tomorrow and insist that I return to the hospital for more testing.

I pulled the pillow off of my face. What a day. I guess I should say what a weekend. It was unreal. "I have amnesia. I have *amnesia*. *I* have amnesia." Nope, saying it a bunch of times in different ways didn't make it feel any less bizarre.

I vowed that from this point on things were going to be different. The next time Carter saw me, he wouldn't recognize the composed and together person I know has to be inside me somewhere. Plus, I had to be hip for my fans. I was some kind of internet sensation these days. I might have some people who look up to me or something. It's possible.

I wanted to brush my teeth, but shelved the idea immediately. I absolutely refused to leave this room again tonight. Lucy peeked out from under the covers. Luckily, she didn't care if I acted idiotically. I didn't have to pretend with her. I didn't have to pretend with Cheryl either. I wanted to call her but since she had just left a few hours ago I decided to suck it up and wait until tomorrow. Anyway, I wanted to talk about what had just happened with Carter. Regardless of how accepting she was about it, I couldn't bring myself to speak with her about him. It was too strange. I could still remember the sixteen year old Carter coming to spend the weekend with us at our house and the two of us making fun of the Goth look he had been trying out. It was okay to laugh at him with her, but talking about kissing him was another matter.

I tried to superimpose the Goth Carter onto Super-Hot Carter but it was almost impossible. Super-Hot Carter was just too powerful, so much so that I could hardly believe they were the same person. That was good I guess. I didn't feel as dirty if I couldn't see him as a kid. My mind went back to the new office décor but I quickly shut it down. I couldn't deal with that tonight.

I should go to sleep. Sitting up thinking about things was only making me more uptight. I would most likely be well by morning, sleeping in my own bed in my own house. I crawled under the covers for the second time tonight, but this time I was going to stay put. I closed my eyes and started counting sheep. After a few seconds of that I became angry. Who came up with that stupid idea? Watching sheep jump doesn't do anything to make me drowsy. I started to count puppies. Aww, they are so cute.

There was a warm hand on my hip and hot breath on my neck. I leaned back into the firm body that was spooning me. I could feel the bulge of his cock on my ass. I wiggled closer.

"Mmm," he groaned in my ear while he slid his hand up to my breast. My own hand reached up to cover his.

"Well good morning to you, too," I whispered scratchily as he tightened his arm around me, pulling me closer. His tongue and lips started an assault on my neck and I shivered, pressing myself into him. I don't know how long we laid there, practically still but for his mouth, before his hand moved back down to my thigh, grasping it and shifting it forward to make space for him. I could

feel his peen nudging my entrance which was already wet and eager. He pushed himself into me at an excruciatingly slow pace.

"Oh Carter," I gasped as I arched my back.

I bolted upright in bed, my breathing shaky. What the *hell* was that? I could still feel Carter's hand holding me and his lips on my neck. Did I just have a sex dream? Holy moly, I never had those. Ever. My heart was beating fast. Like panic attack fast but in a good way and I was still turned on. *Sex dreams are awesome.*

I switched on the lamp and looked over at the clock. 6:42. Way too early for me to be up. I was the proverbial night owl. I had always been lucky that my body preferred the night since that was when I was at the restaurant. I hoped I wasn't some freakish early riser now. That would totally suck. There was nothing as fabulous as being able to be asleep while the rest of the poor working schmoes were already grinding away at their jobs.

I wanted to go back to sleep, but I didn't want to fall back into the dream. Not that it didn't make me feel good though, precisely the opposite. It probably wouldn't be a very good idea to moon over him while unconscious, I might get carried away or something and force myself on him. Then again, I'd already done that.

I finally got up because I really needed to go to the bathroom. I turned on the lamp and the first thing I saw was the picture of Carter and me. I tried to remember when it was taken, but I came up blank. My stomach sank as I realized I still had no memory of the recent past. *Well, this bites.* I had pinned my hopes on sleep recharging my mind, but was obviously going to take something else.

I crawled out of bed dejectedly. I needed to do something constructive today, something that would actively engage my brain. I made it to the door and opened it a crack. It was quiet. Great. I raced to the bathroom and took care of the most pressing business. Uhg, my mouth felt gross. I picked up my space-aged toothbrush and squeezed some toothpaste on it before I turned it on and started scrubbing my teeth, only then did I look up to see what I can only describe as hideous. It was my head. My entire head.

My eyes were red and puffy from last night's crying jag and the bruise on the side of my head had morphed into what looked like a bad makeup job from an old monster movie, all green and brown. My hair was the worst of all. What wasn't sticking to my head in greasy chunks was poking up in a tangled mess. I momentarily stopped brushing my teeth to gaze at myself. I looked like total crap. I hurriedly finished brushing and stripped out of my clothes. A shower was the only prescription for this disease.

I turned the water on and opened the cabinet to make sure my robe was hanging before stripping down and stepping into the steaming spray. I felt instantly better as I lathered up my hair, the smell of my shampoo familiar and comforting. While I conditioned my hair I pulled the razor off of the shelf and shaved my legs—strictly for myself, of course. After I was done and dried off I felt a hundred times better than I felt yesterday.

When I opened the door I was confronted by someone who was the opposite of hideous. Geez, even at the butt-crack of dawn he looked good. How unfair. His hair looked messy, but that wasn't anything out of the ordinary. Everything else looked amazing. I grabbed the lapels of my robe together like a prudish ninny.

"Good morning," I said in my most schoolmarmish voice. "I'm finished; you can have the bathroom now." He didn't say anything, just looked at me and raised his eyebrows. "Excuse me," I murmured as I pushed past him. He smelled like sleep. It was a good smell. I had to get out of there.

"Morning." He actually grunted something that sounded like "horny" but I think that was me projecting. I rushed to my bedroom and closed the door harder than I meant to before grabbing some jeans and a pretty black tunic with silver embroidery. I didn't recognize it, but I was happy to put on something attractive. I needed the confidence boost. Yesterday was a bitch-slap to my mental wellbeing, and I wasn't sure I was going to be able to handle another day like that one.

Today I would be proactive about remembering. I would go through every email and picture I had. There had to be something somewhere that would make everything fall into place. I was an intelligent woman. It shouldn't be that hard to force my mind to dredge up *something* useful. I went back to my closet and pulled out a pair of ballet flats. Cute. I slipped them on and looked down at myself. Nice.

I went back to the bathroom to dry my hair and was happy to see it was empty. Ten minutes later, with dry hair and a bit of makeup to cover some of the bruising I felt pretty good, all things considered.

I smelled coffee and immediately perked up, faintly amazed that I hadn't felt the need for any earlier. Usually, I couldn't function without caffeine first thing. I wasn't surprised to find Carter already sitting at the island with a coffee mug in front of him.

"I made some coffee." He looked up from the book he was reading and I walked over to the coffee maker.

"Thanks." There was already a mug next to the coffee pot. It was my favorite mug, the one I had used every morning since I had moved into this house. *Carter knew that this was my special mug.* I had to put that thought away until later. I poured my coffee and dumped in a mound of sugar. After I took my first sip I turned back to Carter, who was watching me.

"You look nice." He said it with a smile so I was extra glad I had put on something besides my usual tee shirt.

"Thank you." My voice was all breathy.

All I could think about when I looked at him was my dream. I could feel his lips on my neck and his hand on my breast. My nipples sprang to attention before I could help it. This was going to be tough. I knew it would be impossible to actually have sex with him while I was in this state. For one thing, I usually dated a guy for a while before I took it that far, and another, maybe more pertinent to this situation, I didn't think he would go for it. He stopped kissing me last night because he thought I wasn't ready, so I was pretty sure that he wouldn't be inclined to indulge me in sex. Dang it! I needed to implement my plan to be cool like I had decided last night. Sadly, I had no practice being cool so I didn't know what to do. I fell back on the only thing I had.

"Do you want any breakfast?" I made sure my

voice was strong and clear.

"Only if you want to make some, I was going to make do with coffee."

"Omelet okay?" I asked as I pushed off from the counter I was leaning on and made my way over to the refrigerator.

"Great. Do you want any help?"

No. No. No. "Sure." I smiled and grabbed the carton of eggs and leaned back down to see if there were any mushrooms in the drawer. Bingo. I pulled out the bacon and cheese and set everything down on the counter.

"Bacon and mushroom omelet, your favorite," I said triumphantly. I heard Carter gasp from behind me.

"What?"

"You know what my favorite breakfast is." He said it with such awe that it only took me a moment to understand what he was saying.

"Oh my gosh! How did I know that?" My heart started pounding again, but this time it wasn't in fear. It was excitement. Maybe today *was* going to be my lucky day.

Chapter Ten

Carter was beside me in a second. "What else do you remember?" he asked anxiously while latching on to my upper arms.

I thought hard. Hmm. Nothing really. I had no idea where the whole omelet thing had popped up from. I searched my thoughts for any tiny nugget of information, but I just couldn't bring anything to the surface. Carter was searching my face for some kind of recognition, so I just shook my head.

He slowly released my arms. "That's okay, sweetie. It's in there somewhere. This is a great sign. Maybe it will happen while you aren't even trying." He said it while trying to put on a happy face, but the excitement I had felt just a moment ago was already starting to dissipate.

I stared at his face, trying to force my mind to give me just a little more. I looked down at the breakfast ingredients, and for some reason I couldn't even remember making omelets for Carter anymore. That momentary, fleeting thought was already buried back in my subconscious. I wanted to yell in anger and cry in frustration all at the same time. My heartbeat had slowed back down, too, my tiny victory already overshadowed by reality.

"I guess I'll start the food." I didn't feel like eating, but cooking always made me feel better. It was soothing and I needed that desperately, even if I was just going through the motions. I put the bacon on and then felt his arms come around me. I stood still. Part of me wanted to lean into him, but the other part, the part still a tiny bit freaked out, wanted to elbow him in the stomach.

Whoa, that sounded a little vicious. Am I violent now, too? My mind started racing again, just like it did in the hospital. Maybe I did something crappy to someone and this was my punishment. I didn't really know myself, did I? But then, why would Carter want to be with me? He's a good guy. He's helpful in the kitchen, he's good looking, and he is a damn good kisser. He already sounded better than anyone else I can remember dating. Oh, the irony.

Hmm. He smelled good and he hadn't even showered yet. He was still wearing his tee shirt and sweats. That's something else I should add to the plus column. Nice smelling. You never really think about how important that is until you date someone with B.O., but that's another story.

"Justine, we'll get through this. Who knows what you'll remember next?" He released me to grab a bowl for the eggs and I took it from him without saying anything. This morning was really giving my emotions a workout. First the sex dream, then the memory, now back to square one. It was getting pretty hard to take. We stood there silently, cooking our breakfast, and when everything was done we sat at the island and ate it. Well, he ate his while I pushed my food around the plate. All of this pretty much without talking. Strangely, it didn't seem weird. It felt kind of homey.

I stood to clean up after we were finished, but Carter stopped me.

"What would you like to do today?" The question caught me off guard. I had been planning to look through my pictures and email, but now I was thinking about getting out of the house. I needed something relax me; I had had a rough couple of days.

"Um, I hadn't really thought about it. What would I usually do on a Monday?" He paused as if thinking about it.

"I don't really know. I'm usually at work." Well, so much for that avenue of information.

"Maybe we could go to the farmer's market or something. It's a nice day." I looked out the window as I said this and confirmed that the sun was actually out.

"Sure, we could do that." I couldn't tell if he was happy about the prospect or not. "Whatever you want. Today is all about you." He gathered up the dishes and started rinsing them off. I would have helped him, but I didn't really feel like cleaning; I wanted to be lazy and self-indulgent. At least for today. I watched as he put everything away and I quickly occupied myself with staring at my fingernails a second before he turned around.

"I'm going to take a shower; you decide what you want to do." He leaned forward like he was going to kiss me then veered to the side and walked past. What the heck? I was almost expecting contact now.

Lucy was hanging around my feet, waiting for her own breakfast, so I got her some food and watched her while she ate it. Dogs didn't have these kinds of problems. How was I supposed to function in society with only a partial knowledge of my life and even less knowledge of my job?

There was nothing left for me to do in the kitchen, and the only thing I could think to keep myself occupied was straightening up my bed. I had never realized how boring life could get if you didn't have set plans in place. This wasn't like a day off or even a vacation. At least during those times you focused on doing things that *weren't* part of your everyday routine. As I couldn't remember my everyday routine, there wasn't anything in front of me but endless stretches of *nothing*. It made me feel useless.

I heard the shower running as I passed the bathroom door. It didn't take much to start imagining Carter on the other side, naked. It caused a bit of a tingle in my stomach, so I paused there like a creepy stalker, listening for any kind of sound. *Hey, it might help nudge my memory or something.* After a few seconds, when I didn't remember anything helpful, I started to feel slightly dirty, so I went along to the bedroom, straightening the covers and fluffing up my pillows.

By the time I had finished, I heard the shower go off. I didn't want to run into him in the hallway so I sat on the bed, waiting for him to go back out to the kitchen. He didn't. He came out of the bathroom covered only in a towel. I took a breath. Oh. My. God. Literally. We are talking Greek god here. My eyes locked on his chest for the second time in twelve hours. *How on earth do I not remember this?* Why would I want to forget? My eyes drifted lower and I forced myself to look to the side.

"Sorry, I thought you were still in the kitchen." He strolled into the room completely unconcerned that I was sitting there gaping at him. It made me wonder if he usually walked around the house wearing next to nothing. I hoped so. For after I get my memory back, I mean. Right now I was just a perv.

"No problem, let me get out of here so you can get dressed." I hopped up and shot out of the room, closing the door behind me and made my way back to the living room. How had I never noticed how little there was to do in my house? I just went from room to room without any purpose. I missed being needed at the restaurant. I hadn't thought about it much, too many other things to worry about, but now I let the sadness in. I couldn't remember all the stuff Cheryl had told me about happening, but I believed her. It was just hard to realize that I wasn't officially a chef anymore, not in the truest sense of the word. I felt lost.

Carter emerged from the bedroom looking totally put together in a brown pullover and dark wash jeans. "Are you ready to go? It's still early."

I looked at the clock on the wall. It was just after eight. Early for me, anyway. "Yeah, let's get out of here." I walked out the door after grabbing my purse and stopped at the driveway. Should I drive? I didn't really want to, but I thought I should at least offer. "Would you like to go in my car?"

Carter shook his head. "Uh, no that's okay. I hate your driving."

"Excuse me?"

"Well, you punch the gas and mash on the brakes

constantly. I can't relax in the car with you." I wanted to feel insulted, but this was not the first time I had heard those exact words to describe my driving. I decided to be the bigger person and let it slide.

"Fine, you drive. Where are we going?"

"The farmer's market. That's the first thing you said so I figured that's where you really wanted to go." I nodded and waited while he unlocked the car doors.

"I know you probably think it's stupid to want to go there, but we can find something for dinner." I loved the farmer's market, all the choices and all the people. Plus, I couldn't live without the goat cheese from my favorite seller.

"Not at all. I like going there, too. It's full of happy memories." Huh? He has happy memories of the farmer's market? Weirdo.

We sat in silence as he drove down my street and onto busier roads. Everything looked perfectly familiar to me. I felt like my old self. "Thanks. I really needed this." I felt about the farmer's market like other women felt about the spa. Utter relaxation and happiness.

"My pleasure." He smiled back at me and for the first time in days I felt really good. We walked around, looking at what was on offer, which wasn't much since it was a weekday. I walked to a table with an enormous pumpkin in front of it. I had forgotten that it was already autumn, which meant it was closer to Thanksgiving and piles of food. My mood was getting lighter by the minute.

"What would you like me to make tonight? Pick anything here." I was feeling magnanimous as I stretched my arms out to encompass the entire market.

Carter thought for a moment. "Asparagus risotto?"

I nodded and backtracked to the longhaired guy who had the super-thin asparagus that was out of season. "Five pounds, please." It was much more than I needed, but they looked so good I wanted to have some on hand. My mind was already trying to formulate a recipe for the extras. Carter pulled out his wallet to pay for them before I had a chance to and took the bag.

"Thanks." I remembered I only had about fourteen dollars in cash and I wasn't sure if I had anything in the bank. That might have been an embarrassing situation just now. I needed to check out my bank account when we got home.

We walked a little more, but my cheese guy wasn't there, so I made do with the asparagus and we headed back to the car. I was happier than I had felt in days. I reached out for Carter's hand. He looked surprised but took it. I felt an electrical shock run up my arm and I also saw a picture of Carter in my head. I was telling him that I loved him. Oh my god. I was telling Carter I loved him. At the farmer's market.

I stopped walking. "Carter. I just remembered something."

"What?"

"I told you I loved you here." His eyes got wide. He started squeezing my hand almost painfully.

"Yes. It was the first time you ever said it to me. Right over there." He pointed down a few more spaces. My breathing was coming fast.

I told him I loved him for the first time at the farmer's market? Aren't I the romantic fool? I felt slightly embarrassed, but that feeling was far outweighed by the excitement of my memory.

"Let's go home, I want to look at pictures and see if I remember anything else." I tugged him along to his truck, and when we got there he paused before opening my door for me.

"One thing first." He paused and pulled his hand from mine and moved it up to my face. "I love you, Justine." He didn't try to kiss me, but I was too happy to care. I was *remembering*.

I didn't know if I was supposed to say it back. Technically, I wasn't feeling *romantic* love toward him right now. I felt grateful, even extra friendly, but I don't think the lust from this morning would really count as love. I stood there mute. He opened my door still smiling. I guess he wasn't feeling too slighted.

He went around to his side while I sat there trying to dredge up something else. Dammit, I couldn't remember on demand. That's okay, though. I had already remembered two things today and it wasn't even noon. He put the bag on the floor in the small backseat area and got in. He looked happy. Really happy.

"I'm glad we came here," I said as we pulled out. Not only did I spend some time perusing the offerings, but I had to admit I had a good time with Carter. He didn't even complain once at all the time I spent fondling vegetables.

"Me too. I told you I had good memories from here." That's right, he had. I was glad I didn't know what they were earlier; the pressure probably would have prevented me from remembering a thing. We drove home without talking, just like before, but this time I was feeling much more positive.   .

Chapter Eleven

I sat in happy silence. I was happy because, well duh, I was finally remembering some things. Carter was happy, I could only assume, because I remembered where I had told him I loved him for the first time. I wasn't entirely sure how I was feeling about that. I remembered saying the words, but I couldn't feel the emotion behind it. That really sucked. On the plus side, though, I hadn't remembered anything else about my life, but I had already remembered two things regarding Carter.

For the first time since waking up in the hospital, I really wanted to remember my relationship with him. I wanted to remember *being* with him. Age really wasn't coming in to play as the deal breaker I thought it would be. He didn't seem that young to me anymore. He wasn't too young unless you're like fifty. Shoot, even someone fifty years old would find Carter hot. I hadn't thought of him as Cheryl's brother, either, which helped matters immensely.

"Do you want to stop for some lunch?" His voice

interrupted my thoughts. Did I want to eat? Hell yes, remembering was hungry work.

I didn't feel a moment's hesitation about spending time with Carter. I would be a liar if I said that it had nothing to do with thinking about sex with him. I had been thinking about it quite a lot since I woke up this morning. It was unusual. I really didn't think about sex all that much. I mean, I liked having it and all; it just wasn't something I spent too much time worrying about. I had a feeling sex with Carter was going to be something worth thinking about.

"Well?" Carter's impatient voice broke into my musings. I realized that I hadn't answered him out loud.

"Oh, yeah. I could eat something." I wanted to scarf down a few tacos or some French fries, that usually made me feel good, but I didn't want to look like a pig in front of him. For some twisted reason I wanted to appear dainty. I saw a Wendy's up ahead— they served salads! "Why don't we just drive through at Wendy's?"

"Uh, okay." I guess Carter had somewhere else in mind, but I was anxious to get home and look through my pictures. He pulled in and got in line. I looked at the menu board. Mmm, the burgers and fries were calling me, because even though I mostly avoided beef, sometimes the lure of a cheeseburger was just too strong. But I wasn't weak.

"I'll take a plain baked potato and a side salad, please," I told him, proud of myself for sounding sensible and healthful.

He looked at me as if I had grown two heads. "Don't you want the double?"

The double patty cheeseburger sounded divine,

but I didn't want him to know that. He did know my eating preferences, though. I was wavering in my convictions. I didn't want the salad. Well, that's not true; I wanted the cheeseburger and the salad. Decisions, decisions. Hunger beat dignity.

"Yeah, I guess I'll take the double." I tried to make it sound as if I was only getting it to humor him. "Oh, and a Coke."

He ordered two double cheeseburger meals and drove up to the window to pay. I was faced again with my lack of funds, but I did have my fourteen dollars.

"Here, I'll pay for this." I pulled my wallet out of my purse and grabbed my cash. He handed the money to the girl at the window and paid for the food. He handed me the change and then drove forward and took the bag from the teenaged boy in the next window. "Extra ketchup, please," I told him before it was too late and we drove away. He put the drinks in the cup holders and handed me a huge wad of ketchup packets. The smell of food was permeating the car, and by the time he parked and we gathered the food and the asparagus and carried it in, I was ravenous. He grabbed some plates and I separated the junk food feast between the two of us.

I politely waited until he sat down before tearing into my food. After I had eaten most of my fries I moved on to my burger at a ladylike pace. That's when I remembered my money situation. I had to know if I was on the brink of bankruptcy or if I was finally financially comfortable.

"Do I have any money?" He finished his bite before answering me.

"What do you mean, exactly?"

I was embarrassed to have to ask, but it was vitally important to me to know what I was dealing with. "I need to know how much money I have available. Do you know?"

"Well, not down to the penny, but yeah, I have a pretty good idea. Do you need something? You should have told me."

"I was just wondering. I only had fourteen dollars in my wallet, and I wasn't sure if I had any money in the bank or anything." I didn't want to admit to Carter that since I bought the house, money had been tight. I always managed to pay the mortgage and keep the electricity on, but often I was glad to be able to eat at the restaurant.

"You're doing great. Your website is very popular. If you want, you can check online."

"Right." I hadn't even thought about checking online. I could have saved myself a lot of embarrassment. "Thanks." We finished eating and I threw all the trash away. I wanted to look through my photo albums, but I needed to know my financial picture first.

I left Carter in the kitchen and went straight to the office computer. I was jarred by the furnishings again as I grabbed a pen out of a hairy Chewbacca mug on my desk, ready to jot down my balance. I pulled up my bank online, but it didn't let me into my account. I tried again. Denied. I was getting frustrated. I typed in my information one more time. It sent me to a page that told me I was being locked out for security reasons. Great, now I was on some kind of a hackers list or something. I banged my fist down on the keyboard. Carter picked that moment to walk in.

"What's wrong?" He came and looked over my shoulder. "What did you do?"

"I don't know. It wouldn't accept my information." I was feeling angry and embarrassed, all my happiness from earlier had evaporated with my money and technology problems.

He leaned over me and looked closer. "This isn't even your bank, Justine."

"Yes it is. I've always banked here." I think I know my own bank.

"Not anymore. You bank at First National now. You have for the past six months. We both have. They opened a branch right around the corner."

It stuck me again that he knew things I had no idea about. "Can you help me check?"

"Sure." I hopped up and he took the chair before digging in the desk drawer and pulling out a check book. I looked closely at it, it was mine. He typed in the account numbers and password.

"How do you know my password?"

He smirked at me. "You told me. It's sexyCarter1."

I felt my face flame. I felt like I was in middle school and the cute boy I had a crush on found a note I wrote about him.

"Don't worry, I picked something equally cheesy."

"Hmm." That was highly doubtful. I waited while my information popped up but I couldn't believe what I was seeing. There, right before my eyes was $7,344.19. That was impossible.

"What is this?" Carter must have typed in his own information.

"Your checking account."

No way, there was no way that was correct. "That can't be right. That's too much."

"It is. I told you your website is popular. I wasn't exaggerating. You are doing *very* well. Once you get the advance for the cookbook, you'll be doing even better."

Omigod. I'm *rich*. Well, maybe other people wouldn't think seven thousand dollars was much, but as far as I was concerned, I was loaded.

"Anything else you need to know?" I knew I was grinning like a fool. I just shook my head. Wow. Not only am I kind of famous, I'm rich, too. Oh yeah, and I have a hot boyfriend. The only downside was that I couldn't remember any of this. But on the upside I was now one of *those* people. The kind of person that other people envy.

I took a moment to glory in my newfound awesomeness. I didn't know what I should do next. I wanted to go look at some pictures or something, but I also wanted to laze around and think about how good things were going in the life that I couldn't remember.

"Nah, I'm good." Dang right I'm good. I've finally arrived. "Do we have some photos I could look at? I already looked at the book beside the bed. I was hoping something would click, but unfortunately nothing did."

He nodded. "There are some on here." He motioned to the computer. "Plus, I think you have a bunch on your phone." Oh yeah, I had forgotten my phone, I probably have some cool stuff on there.

"Well, let's look at them. You can tell me when and where and everything."

"Okay." He opened a folder marked "Pictures."

Hmm, you'd think I would have noticed that since it was on the desktop and all.

I pulled his stool from his drafting table and perched on it right next to him. He started going through the pictures one by one. There were a lot of shots with no humans, just mountains and snow.

"These are from when we went skiing in Colorado." I went skiing? Who is this new me? I must not be as clumsy as I remember. Nice.

I sat in silence as other pictures came up. Me alone, Carter alone, the two of us together at some party. Oh, those are from Cheryl's house. I placed my hand on top of Carter's to make him pause. I got that same jolt as earlier, but I didn't have a new flash of memory. I looked closer at the picture. It was obviously taken by someone else because Carter and I were looking at each other with what can only be described as heat. I got a tingle in my belly. I wanted to remember that moment. I realized I still had my hand on Carter's so I pulled it away.

He moved on to the next pictures. Nothing looked familiar to me. I was becoming frustrated again. I must have made some sound because Carter turned to me, placing his face mere inches from mine. I couldn't move. The only thing I could do was take a deep breath. His scent hit me like a ton of bricks. Suddenly, I did have a memory. I was sniffing Carter, but we weren't wearing any clothes. We weren't sitting upright either. His smell triggered a memory of sex and my body was suddenly craving it. It's like my body remembered what my mind refused to. I leaned into him, like I had in the kitchen, but this time I wasn't embarrassed by it; I was turned on. There was only one thing to do in this situation. My mouth had a mind of its own.

"Can we have sex?"

Chapter Twelve

Omigod, did that just come out of my mouth? I sat still in mortification, but on the inside I was churning. *Please say yes. Please say yes.*

He jerked his head back so that he could look at me. "What?" I didn't answer him. He heard me, and I wasn't brave enough to repeat it. "Justine, I don't think it's a good idea." He used the voice of someone trying to let you down gently. "Not that I don't want to."

Yeah right, I've heard that before. Really, I have. Unfortunately, this was not the first time I had been turned down for sex. However, it was the first time I had been rejected by someone who supposedly loved me. My sense of humiliation increased tenfold with that thought. I had to get out of here.

I made to hop off my stool but he grabbed my arm and wouldn't let me escape.

"Uh uh. You're not going to say something like that and run away. Why do you want to have sex with me? Right now?"

I didn't want to tell him what I had just remembered, but I realized if I didn't I would be denied for sure.

"I just had a flash of memory when I smelled you. I could remember us in bed." He widened his eyes and waited for me to continue. "I was sniffing you just now and I could see us, naked, in bed." I was embarrassed to tell him this. Once again it made me seem like I had some kind of sniffing fetish.

His eyes had changed. First they were taken by surprise, then interest, now they were filled with lust. Oh yeah, he wanted me. My ego re-inflated, and I wanted to gloat, but there was no time. I felt like a squirming, melting mess.

"Justine, when we are together like that again, I want you to know it's me. I need you to *know* me."

For butt's sake, how could he turn down an offer of sex? I only had a fleeting memory, but I could see we were hot together. It wasn't right. Not only was I currently being denied my life, but I was also being denied a necessary part of human companionship in the form of scorching hot intercourse.

I took my hands off his shoulders and stood up.

"Wait. Juss, wait."

I didn't listen, instead scurrying into the bedroom and closing the door. I flopped down on the bed. I felt horribly lonely. It was strange; spending the morning with Carter had been great, I felt comfortable for the first time in two days. I wanted to spend *more* time with him. I couldn't help the fact that I wanted to be with him. I guess the real problem was that my hormones had gone into overdrive and I had ended up propositioning him like a street walker.

So, here I was, back on the bed, writhing in humiliation. It's like some kind of sick pattern. I wanted to leave the house and drive around or something, but I didn't have anywhere to go. I thought about Cheryl. Of course! I could go to her house. I just couldn't tell her what happened. Some things were even too embarrassing to share with your best friend. I sat up, ready to get my phone and call her. I had only gotten as far as the thought of leaving when the bedroom door opened.

"Please leave," I said politely. "I could use a little time on my own."

"I've got a better idea. You said you smelled me and remembered. Try it again."

"What?" Uh, *no*.

"Smell me." He said it quietly, but it was a command.

I looked over at him. He had pulled his long sleeved shirt off, so all he had on was a form fitting white tee shirt and his jeans. He looked positively edible. My mind drove me right back to downtown Lustville.

"I don't know." I was afraid of getting all worked up again and then being shoved aside like some humping puppy. I was in a precarious state of mind. I didn't need the rejection.

"Come on Justine, you know you want to." He sounded like a drug pusher. He knew I needed a fix. I could only hold out for so long. He sat next to me.

"All right. One sniff, then I'm leaving." Even to my own ears this conversation sounded bizarre. I leaned over and smelled his tee shirt. Damn, he smelled delicious. I closed my eyes and really let myself get into it.

He moaned and his arm came up around my waist. *I'll take that as a good sign.* I pulled my hands up to his shoulders to steady myself and got up on my knees. He didn't move, but his eyes closed. Mmhmm. I was going to get some.

I threw one knee over his thighs so that I was straddling him. I tilted my head so that I could smell his neck, and I couldn't stop my tongue from touching his skin. It was slightly salty, but it just turned me on more. My lips moved from his neck to his jaw, never breaking contact. I placed my hand on either side of his head, about to connect with his mouth, when I felt myself being flipped down onto my back on the bed.

He was on top of me in an instant kissing me with a passion he had obviously been holding back yesterday.

"Justine." He whispered it into my mouth. I felt good. No, good is too tame, I felt great. My skin felt electric.

My hands went sliding under his shirt, making contact with the smooth skin of his stomach. I felt his muscles tense under my fingertips. That wasn't all I felt. I could feel the hard bulge of his peen pressing into my thigh. I did a happy dance in my head. Yay for me! I moved my legs to press against it and he groaned. I could feel it all down my body.

"Please Carter, please." I didn't like to beg, but desperate times and all that.

He pulled his head back and opened his eyes. "Take your shirt off." *Yes.* Now we were getting somewhere. I moved out from under him slightly while I pulled the tunic off, sorry that I had a bra on. He popped open the clasp with his beautiful long fingers and cupped my left breast all the while pushing us back down onto the mattress. Before I could take another breath, he had his mouth attached to my right breast, causing a tingle all the way down to my toes.

I laid there like a slug, just moaning and squirming, waiting for him to really get down to business when two things happened at once. Lucy started barking ferociously and the doorbell chimed. No, Nooooo! I wanted to put my hands over Carter's ears, but it was too late. He stopped what he was doing, what I was secretly starting to believe he was born to do, and sat up quickly. I continued to lie there, prostrate, in a stupor of yearning.

He paused, and I assumed he was waiting to see if whoever was at the door decided to leave. No such luck. The evil troll at the front door decided to mash on the bell again and Carter jumped up.

"Don't answer it," I hissed from my prone position.

"I have to. It might be something important." *This* wasn't important?

He grabbed my tunic from the floor where I had thrown it only a minute before, in that wonderful time when I was on the fast track to satisfaction. I took it, but not without glaring at Carter first. He just gave me a look like Ralphie from *A Christmas Story* that said "But the bell rang," and turned toward the door. The doorbell chimed again and my frustration got the better of me.

"Hold on. We're busy right now!" I screamed this at the top of my lungs and pulled my top on. Carter disappeared to the living room.

Lucy had stopped barking and had barreled into the bedroom and retrieved her stuffed duck. Must be someone she knows at the door. She always had to show off her toys to her friends. Friend or not, I would not be appeased. Whoever it was just spoiled what was gearing up to be quite the afternoon.

"What took you so long?" I could hear Cheryl's voice twinkling down the hallway and I was torn. Twenty minutes ago I was going to call her, I was looking forward to seeing her. Now, not so much.

I couldn't hear Carter's reply. I'm sure he wasn't telling her the holdup, though. It just didn't seem like something he would do. I made my way out to the living room; I had to be sociable since she was my best friend. Carter smoothed down my hair and gave me a strange look.

Cheryl's eyes were moving between the two of us with raised eyebrows. I looked down at myself and saw that my shirt was on inside out. I wanted to fix it, but I decided to brazen it out. I didn't know what to say and I guess the two of them didn't either. We stood there in awkward silence for about fifteen seconds before Carter stepped into the void.

"Cheryl, did you need something?"

"Not really. I just came to visit with Justine for a while." She walked over to the couch and plopped herself down. Lucy jumped up and joined her. It didn't look like she was leaving any time soon. Crap. My desire was slowly seeping away. I let go of Carter's arm and joined Cheryl on the couch.

"I remembered some things today," I told her while I made myself comfortable and put my feet on the coffee table.

"Ooh, like what?" She was like a schoolgirl, giddy and anxious.

"Well, first thing this morning, I remembered Carter loves bacon and mushroom omelets. Then, at the farmer's market, I remembered telling him I loved him for the first time."

"Oh, I love your bacon and mushroom omelets," she said wistfully. Obviously, my news came in a distant second. She finally clued in. "Oh, Justine that's awesome. See, everything is going to come back, just like they said." She leaned forward and pulled me into a hug. "And it's only been two days!"

"I know. I'm finally starting to believe everything is going to be okay."

Carter sat down on the loveseat looking disgruntled. Good, now he knew how I was feeling just a little while ago. I wished Cheryl would leave so that we could continue our previous activities out here. It wouldn't be the first time.

I thought back to when Cheryl had walked in on us inflagranti delicto. Her screams were only drowned out by Carter's. I laughed. As embarrassing as it was, it was also hilarious. Wait. I just remembered that. Holy Frack! I remembered! My adrenaline was pumping. Things were flying back to me so fast. This was the third thing today. No, the fourth. I jumped off of the couch and they both looked up at me in surprise.

"I just remembered. I remembered you walking in on us, Cheryl!" I was so excited I could hardly keep myself from jumping up and down. I went over to the loveseat and grabbed Carter's arm. "I remembered." He looked up at me with a mixture of happiness and mortification. He started blushing but I just grinned back. Then, slowly, the embarrassment started to creep into my thoughts. I hardly remembered anything, but I remembered being caught having sex with my best friend's younger brother. *Before* we had gone public. I recalled that much. Now I was blushing, too. I felt like we had just been caught again. I let go of Carter's arm and sat back down on the couch, wishing the floor would swallow me up.

Carter looked angry. "Cheryl, I don't mean to be rude, but could you please leave. I think Justine and I need to talk."

Chapter Thirteen

He *was* angry. *What did I do?*

I jumped up. "Cheryl, you don't have to leave."

Cheryl glanced from me to Carter, this time I followed her gaze and saw Carter giving her a very pointed look.

"Uh, Juss, I need to be getting home, anyway. You call me. Anytime." She left as quickly as she'd come, but Carter and I were in a completely different situation than when she arrived. We stood there like two combatants, but I didn't know what we were going to fight about.

"I am not going to go through all that again. It was hard enough the first time."

I had no idea what he was talking about. What did we go through? I looked at him and waited for him to elaborate. When he didn't I had to ask.

"Carter, I don't know what you are talking about. What have we gone through that was hard? I have amnesia, remember?"

He took a breath before answering me. "What just happened. You being embarrassed about me. I am not going to go through that again. I know you don't realize how it hurts me, but it does, Justine. I

126

don't want to be some dirty secret to you. I won't be."

I looked at him in horror. I didn't think of him as a dirty secret. True, I was embarrassed just now in front of Cheryl, but that was mainly from the memory itself, not Carter's part in it. Okay, it was partly because of him. What did he expect? He is my best friend's brother. And he *is* four years younger than me. It wasn't as big a deal as when he was a teenager, but I've still got that picture in my head. I couldn't help it. Plus, over the years I had gotten really close with both of his parents, and that just added on a layer of self-consciousness around them. Call me crazy, but I felt closer to them than my own mother, and it was a tough thing to be "the girlfriend" to their son instead of just me.

I shook my head. "It's not like that. I promise. I was just thinking about her walking in on us. It *was* embarrassing, Carter. You know that. I remember enough to know that. It wasn't any better for you."

He just looked at me. I could see a little of his anger was draining. "So you're not embarrassed to be seen with me? It's not *weird*?" Ugh. He was asking me something that, if I answered truthfully, he wasn't going to like. My only other option was to lie. I chose to tell him the truth. I had enough things going on with everything else right now; I didn't need to add another layer on top.

"Maybe just a little bit, but it's not you, it's me." I could see he was trying to butt in, so I held my hands up. "Try to see things from my point of view, please."

He leaned back on the cushion. "I've already done that. We have had this conversation before. Do you want me to give you a rehash of what happened?" He raised his eyebrows to me.

"What do you mean?"

"I mean look around, I live here. With you. You are my girlfriend. You got over it." Hmm. He might have a point there, but it was still new to *this* me. *I* hadn't gotten over anything.

"I can't help how I feel, Carter. It's not fair of you to make me feel bad about it. This is still new to me." Carter closed his eyes and took a deep breath before he looked at me again.

"I know. I'm sorry." I waited for him to continue but he didn't.

"I'm remembering things, please be patient. I don't want to mess something up because I don't know what may or may not have happened between us."

He got up and walked over to me. "You're right. It's a sore subject with me." He paused and gave me a saucy grin. "So, what exactly did you remember just now?"

I could feel the blush blooming. I didn't want to tell him, and when he started laughing I knew he didn't need me to tell him anything. "How can you laugh? It was very humiliating."

"Hey, you were laughing when you remembered. It's only fair I can laugh now. Anyway, you're right. It's funny in retrospect, but at the time it was horrible. But the look on Cheryl's face was priceless." We chuckled as we thought about that moment and I felt the warm fuzzies in my stomach. We did have a shared history, even if I couldn't fully remember it at the moment.

He was still standing directly in front of me and I thought about what we had been doing before Cheryl showed up. I looked down at my inside out shirt. Oh my god. I couldn't remember feeling like this before. I think I might have become some kind of sex-crazed hussy. I think I like it. I had never been the kind of person who spent a lot of time thinking about sex, or seeking it out for that matter, but being around Carter was turning me into that kind of girl. I didn't have a problem with it at all. Hell, I'd made a career out of it.

"So, what do you want to do for the rest of the day?" Carter's voice interrupted my musings. I wanted to say "have sex," but I didn't think that's what he had in mind.

"I don't know. I picked the market earlier, why don't you choose?" I hoped he wouldn't choose something outside because I didn't really want to leave the house. I felt comfortable here.

"Do you want to play a game?" My mind went straight to strip poker.

"What do you have in mind?" Strip poker, strip poker.

"Monopoly?" Strip Monopoly?

"What?"

Shit, did I just say that out loud? I tried to play it off. "Huh?"

He looked at me with a raised brow. "Did you just say strip Monopoly?"

I wracked my brain for any words that sounded like strip that I could pass off. Rip, grip, lip, snip. Nothing. They all sounded stupid. I had to fess up.

"Maybe."

"Well, I was just thinking about playing it the regular way, but if you feel the need to be more comfortable..." He left off without finishing.

I shook my head; my tunic was working well for

me today, except that it was still inside out. Maybe a tee shirt was in order.

"Actually, I think I will go put something else on. You get out the game." I went to my bedroom closet and looked through it. I grabbed a tee shirt at random and ripped off my tunic. My bra was still hanging on my shoulders but gaping open in the front, so I pulled it off and threw it on the bed before I pulled on the tee. It was a little big but it felt good so I left it on and went back into the living room. Carter had the board out and was divvying up the money when I walked in.

"You want Leia, right? I'll be Obi-Wan Kenobi." He looked up while holding up the piece. My eyes shot down to the board. Freaking Star Wars Monopoly, of course. I wasn't even surprised.

"Sure." I actually sucked at Monopoly, always had, but maybe Princess Leia would lead me to victory.

He placed the pieces on the starting space and sat on the floor on one side of the coffee table. I took the side by the couch and sat down opposite him. This was kind of weird. A half hour ago I was on the cusp of getting lucky and now I was sitting on the floor playing a board game. A girl really couldn't count on anything.

"Do you want to go first?" I thought it would be a nice touch to be charitable.

"Okay." He picked up the dice and it was game on. I was totally caught up, feeling cutthroat and aggressive. It wasn't the usual me at all. Unfortunately, I was still way behind. Carter had the Death Star and a butt load of settlements while I was stuck with the ghetto spaces. On my next turn I landed on one of his cities, and it wiped me out.

"Suck that!" His gloating got my ire up.

"Uhg, next time we are playing Scrabble, I told you I wasn't playing this with you anymore. It's no fun to always lose." I tossed my money onto the board and scooted up off the floor and onto the couch. Yeah, I know I'm a bad sport.

Carter was up and at my side in an instant. "See Juss, it's all coming back." He plopped down next to me and pulled me into a hug. It took me a moment to understand what he meant.

"The game. We've played the game before." I couldn't actually remember playing Monopoly with Carter, but I could remember being disgruntled. That was something anyway. I let him hug me even though it was causing my loins to stir afresh. Who was I to turn down spontaneous affection?

My stomach growled and I looked at the clock. I couldn't believe it was already after five. We must have been playing for hours. I pulled back and looked at Carter's face. I needed to eat something so that I could keep my hands and mouth occupied. It wasn't safe to leave me to my own devices just yet. Maybe there was something to the whole smoking thing.

"So you want asparagus risotto, right?"

"Yep. Does that still sound good to you?"

"Sure. I love it." He made no move to get up so I just sat there, too. I was feeling pretty relaxed, not tongue-tied or anything. It was kind of a big deal for me. I leaned back onto the arm of the couch. I could see myself lounging around the house with Carter. I knew him well enough to not have to try too hard. I still had that little feeling niggling inside me that there was something I was blocking, but it was being drowned out by other, better feelings. Maybe if I quit fighting my natural instincts, everything would snap back into place.

"Justine, I love you. I just want you to know that." He said the words as nonchalantly as if he were asking me to pass him the remote. He didn't make any move to touch me and I was unsure of what to say to him. My mind wasn't trying to fight his words like before. I knew now that he did love me, and after my revelation on the sidewalk this morning, I knew I loved him even if I couldn't feel it, presently. A part of me wanted to say it back, just so he could feel better, but I realized it wouldn't be right. What could I do? I had a very limited skill set when it came to these situations. Things were complicated.

I was suddenly struck with inspiration. "Carter, I've been having all these memories today and they all center around you. Do you think maybe you could just lean over here and kiss me or something?" The way I said it made it sound stupid. "I mean, maybe kissing you would help me to remember more. You know?" I couldn't look at him when I asked him to kiss me so I looked at his crotch. After a second I noticed he hadn't answered me so I looked into his face.

He wasn't looking at me. Well, he was looking at me but not my face. He was staring at my boobs. "Carter, did you hear me?" He was looking at my boobs and he wasn't even a pervert, not that I knew of anyway.

He didn't answer me but he did lean over from his cushion and put his hands on both sides of my face. I took a deep breath because I knew he was about to kiss me and I didn't want to interrupt things by having to gasp for air. His lips touched mine so lightly I wasn't sure if I was imagining it at first. He pressed in a little harder and I knew it was real. My heart started beating hard again, just like it had the first time.

"I love you." He whispered it when he changed position and I couldn't help it, my legs parted on their own. "I love you so much." Was he trying to kill me? My own hands went up to his arms and I grabbed on. We were just kissing, but it was *hot*. My leg came up and over his thigh and tried to anchor him to me. For once I didn't feel clumsy or uncoordinated, I felt like a goddess. I wanted to feel like this every second of the day. I just wanted to remember. If this was how it felt to be with Carter, I wanted to remember it.

He moved from my lips to my ear. "Please remember me." All the air left my lungs in a whoosh. I would have given up my cool new life to remember him right then, but all I could remember was one word and it didn't seem to fit the occasion.

Chapter Fourteen

"Kumquat."

Carter jerked up and practically off of me. "What did you say?" His eyes were searching mine.

"Kumquat?" I said it like a question. "Why? What does it mean?"

"Are you sure you don't have any idea?"

Duh, I just asked didn't I? "No. It just popped into my head. Why would I be thinking of a fruit? It doesn't make any sense to me."

I could tell Carter was deciding whether to tell me or not, but I wasn't about to let him withhold information that could be crucial to my recovery.

"It's our secret code." Our secret code? Did we make our own club?

"Secret code for what?"

"Sex." He sounded like he was embarrassed but I wasn't. My mind was obviously at a place where Carter wasn't letting my body go.

"We have a secret code for sex?" Hmm. It sounded like we were a little kinky. I wasn't sure how to take that. Do we somehow use kumquats? I really don't like kumquats, they're too tart.

He was blushing again. Wow, he was almost as prone to them as I was.

"Carter, why do we need a code word?"

"It's just a little thing we do, it's no big deal." He tried to dismiss it, but I raised my eyebrows so that he would continue. "Sometimes if we're out and there are other people around it might go like "Do you want a kumquat?" and no one else will know what we're talking about. It's not like we are constantly using that word in public. We actually use it more around the house. It's one of our things. It's only for us." His explanation gave me a warm feeling inside and not just inside my loins. We had cutie couple phrases. That was awesome.

I smiled at Carter. "I want a kumquat." He raised his brows.

"What about dinner? I thought we were going to have some risotto, and you know how long it takes."

I could tell he was trying to brush me off, but he was weakening. I was determined to wear him down. I was afraid if we got up off the couch right now we were not going to be back in this position any time today. That was unacceptable. I was going to have to have some satisfaction. Today.

I wanted to demand sex from Carter. He was obviously waiting for my memory to come back and I could understand his position; he was a standup guy, blah blah blah. The thing was, I no longer felt like he was just Cheryl's brother, someone I hardly knew. I had remembered enough to know that we were an item. A pretty hot ticket. Truthfully, and I'm not a slut or anything, but I have had sex on the first date before. More than once. To guys I knew less than

Carter, the old Carter I mean. Granted, things never really turned out well, but I blame that more on the guys themselves as opposed to the sex. Really. Admittedly, the sex had left something to be desired, but I just couldn't see bad sex between Carter and me. Not if my dream was any indication.

He looked torn. Come *on* man, how tough of a choice is it? Rice or hot sex? It wasn't even close in my opinion. My leg was still wrapped around his thigh, so I pulled myself up to make contact, intimate contact, and I could feel that he was ready.

He dropped his head down to my shoulder and groaned. "Justine, I had a plan for tonight. I wanted things to go in some kind of order. I know you probably don't believe me since I'm lying here on top of you, but it's true."

"I believe you, Carter. I'm sure whatever you have planned will be lovely, but I want a kumquat. Now." That was about as forceful as I was going to get, so if he turned me down, it was all over. I had to pull out the only thing I had left, and even as I said it, I thought it might be true. "It might help me remember."

He looked up and straight into my eyes. "Will you still make risotto?" Holy moly. *He was going to give in*, but the man must really love risotto. I would make a seven course dinner if he wanted. I tried to dial down my excitement a notch. I didn't want to look overeager; I was an adult after all.

"Sure. It does sound good." He looked at me for a second longer and shut his eyes. When he opened them he had a different look in them. He was determined. It gave me a tingle.

He gave me a soft kiss on the side of my mouth

before he opened his and licked the seam of my lips. My mouth opened to him as if it had been waiting for him forever. My hands finally moved from his arms to grasp his back, pulling him even closer to me.

I felt his pelvis grind into mine as he changed position to move us to our sides. His hand molded my waist underneath my shirt while he moved his knee up and between my legs until he settled and I pressed myself down hard before clamping my legs together, holding him in place.

He moved his head so that he could kiss my neck. I couldn't hold back a whimper; I was practically quivering with need. Never had I felt this much desire for anyone. I hardly recognized myself. I put my hand on his hip, really just to anchor myself since I was almost on the edge of the couch, but I couldn't stop myself from moving it up and along his ribcage. His muscles contracted under my fingers infusing me with a bravery that I wasn't used to.

"Help me." I barely whispered the words as I tried to pull his shirt up and off. He didn't even hesitate, taking his hand off me to grab the hem of his shirt and yank it over his head. My head was swimming, I felt a little bit like I did when I woke in the hospital. I couldn't catch a full breath, and what I was managing to suck into my lungs was ragged. The taut muscles of his chest were perfection. His eyes were smoldering emeralds, *yeah, I said it*. It was almost too much for me to take. It was too intense. I wanted to screw my eyes shut and be a coward, leaving everything on a superficial level but it was already too late. I felt like I could see into his soul and it scared me. He wanted to devour me.

Everything was taking on a dreamlike quality. I

moved my mouth to lay a kiss on his chest and his breath whooshed out against my hair. I opened my mouth and swirled the tip of my tongue against his nipple. His arms wrapped around me again and I let myself wallow in the feeling of security, but I couldn't delve too deeply into those emotions right now. I was burning up.

I pulled my mouth off of Carter's chest as he sat up. "Come on." He stood up and tugged me up with him. I didn't say anything as he drew me along to the bedroom; I didn't think I would have been able to, anyway. When we got to bed he turned me so that my back was to it before moving us backward. The moment my legs touched the mattress I dropped down bringing a shirtless Carter with me.

"Wait. Let me get this off." I squirmed out from under him so that I could pull the tee shirt off, leaving us chest to chest. He propped himself on his elbow so that his glorious fingers could work the snap of my jeans. He had the zipper down in a second before sitting up all the way to pull them down. I lifted my hips so they slid down and off easily. I felt suddenly vulnerable, lying there in only my sopping panties and I went to cover my breast with my arm.

"No don't," he said quietly while shaking his head. I stopped with my arm half across my stomach. I was frozen, mesmerized by him, and I couldn't see anything but his eyes. He leaned forward and captured my head with his hands. "You're beautiful."

Gulp. I sat there motionless while he stood up and stripped off his own jeans and boxers. My breath caught in my throat as his peen sprang up from under the elastic band. I couldn't look away and I didn't want to. Oh. My. God. I knew my eyes must have widened, but Carter didn't mention it as he crawled back and over me, cutting off my visual.

When I took a deep breath all I could smell was Carter. It happened to be the most potent thing I had ever encountered. He was kneeling beside my legs and he hooked his fingers around the top of my panties and slipped them off of me. We were both breathing heavily, and my heart pounded against my ribs.

His hands were on my thighs, drawing them slightly apart so that he could put his own knee in the space between. Once I realized what he was doing I pulled my knees up and spread my legs so that he could fit inside them. He bent forward, resting his weight on his hands that were on either side of my head. Seconds later his lips touched my neck and I arched up, I couldn't believe how sensitive my skin felt. I moaned as he moved down to circle my own nipple, pulling it into his mouth and causing a tugging sensation in my womb.

He moved lower, raining kisses down my stomach and to the juncture of my thighs. When he positioned himself there and touched my clit with his tongue my eyes flew open and I looked down. It was the exact picture I had in my head yesterday when I was imagining him kissing me. I guess that had been a memory too, but when he started stroking me with his tongue I couldn't think anymore. I could feel the orgasm building while he used his hands to hold my upper thighs still as I bucked against his mouth.

"Oh my god." I couldn't hold back against the most intense orgasm I could remember. Even as it was overtaking me I felt Carter move up and position himself at my entrance, surging into me a moment later. I cried out as I was overcome with sensation and I could feel myself contracting around him as he plunged in again and again. All I could do was wrap my arms around him and hold on as I exploded. After what felt like an eternity of sensation I felt him stiffen and groan as he had his own release.

He relaxed his arms, lowering himself back down on top of me and as I felt his weight cover me I opened my eyes. "I love you, Carter." I wasn't just saying it because I had just had mind-blowing sex. I said it because I knew it was true down to the tip of my toes.

Chapter Fifteen

I knew without a doubt that I loved him, I could feel it. My heart started beating furiously when I saw the look on Carter's face. He looked so happy that I felt guilty. Yes, I loved him, but I immediately recognized that I still didn't remember all the time it took to build up to that love. That was all missing. I didn't know what else to say. Really, what could follow that?

"I love you, Justine." I tried to smile but I'm not sure if it came across the right way. Now that my sex buzz was wearing off, I was coming to realize I may have acted too hastily in sharing my feelings with Carter. I stayed under him for about thirty seconds before the tension took over and took advantage of his position to scoot out from under him. My nakedness suddenly felt awkward, so I covered my breast with my arm.

I could see the change in Carter's eyes immediately. I sat up on the edge of the bed with my back to him and grabbed for my tee shirt, pulling it on so that I could escape the bedroom.

"I like it when you wear my clothes." His hand

snaked over my still naked hip as he said it, and I couldn't help the goosebumps that broke out on my arms and legs. I looked down and noticed for the first time that there was Darth Vader with "Who's your daddy?" written underneath. I hadn't realized it was his shirt when I put it on, but I guess it only made sense given how baggy it was on me. I searched the floor for my panties but I couldn't see them anywhere. After a few seconds of looking around I decided to grab a fresh pair and pulled open my underwear drawer only to remember it was Carter's now.

He jumped up from the bed and made it to my side in a second.

"Here, this is your drawer." He pulled open the drawer right next to it for me and grabbed a pair of his own boxers out before shoving his drawer closed. *Okay.* Apparently he had privacy issues about his underwear. I found that strange since he jumped up naked to show me my own.

"Thanks." I took out a pair of panties and yanked them on awkwardly, thankful that I was wearing a shirt that fell lower than my butt.

"So, how about dinner?" I asked, trying to extricate myself from the bedroom. Everything seemed to be back to square one. I felt nearly as ill at ease as I had in the hospital. The feeling of closeness and relaxation from earlier had been completely wiped out by my own stupid hormones. I wanted to kick myself. At least earlier, when I was feeling comfortable around him, I was remembering things. The sex hadn't done a thing for my memory.

He was still standing right beside me, naked, so I bolted over to the closet to grab some Capri's, pulling them on at breakneck speed. I wondered how long I was going to have to deal with this self-conscious feeling, knowing it was my own fault. I had practically begged him to have sex with me. Uhg. I turned around to find Carter pulling his jeans back on. A tiny sliver of me was sad that all that beauty was being covered, but mainly I was happy he was dressed; it would make the rest of the evening go so much more smoothly.

"So...dinner?" I asked again.

"Sure. I'll be in to help you in just a minute."

"No rush. I'll just go get things started." This was worse than I thought. We were acting like strangers after a one night stand. Where were the people who went to the farmer's market this morning?

I pulled out the bag of asparagus from the refrigerator, dumping them into my largest colander and rinsing them with cold water. Maybe I should have used cold water to snap me out of my rash behavior a few minutes ago. I wanted to block everything out of my mind and let myself get absorbed in the cooking process, but I had to plan out my meal first. As I was standing at the sink and looking out the window I had an urge to make chocolate mousse. Chocolate always made everything better. I went to the pantry and made sure I had some dark chocolate before snatching it up. I tore open the wrapper and broke off two squares and shoved them into my mouth like medicine, tossing the rest onto the counter. Within a few minutes I had all the ingredients out and the chocolate was melting. I had finished the mousse and was dividing it into four dishes when Carter finally walked in with damp hair. My stomach did a slow roll and I clenched my legs together. Hold it together, Justine.

He looked at the mousse and gave me a curious look without saying anything. "Do you not like mousse?" I asked.

"No, I love it. What made you make this?"

"It just sounded good." He nodded and walked around the island to stand by the sink.

"Do you want me to trim the asparagus?" He looked at me questioningly. I felt I had to do something to break the tension I had caused, so I decided that interacting with him might be a good idea. I had to admit that I was feeling comfortable with him now, after-sex weirdness notwithstanding. I don't know if it was all the memories coming back or if somehow my mind just *knew* him. Either way, I figured I should take the first step.

I looked at the huge pile of asparagus. *What had I been thinking to get so much?* "We can do it together, make it go faster." He smiled and I felt better immediately.

We stood there snapping stems for a few minutes, not speaking, but it wasn't so bad. I was getting over the after sex embarrassment, so things were pretty good in my head. That was until I picked up a stalk as thin as a stick of incense. Ooh, a baby slipped in here. A baby. My mind immediately went into full meltdown mode.

"Shit. You didn't wear a condom," I yelped at him accusingly. My stomach dropped. I didn't even know where in my cycle I was right now. My heart started hammering in my chest. This hadn't even happened to me in high school.

"It's okay, you get the shot. I'm not an idiot." Oh my god, was he implying that *I* am an idiot since I

144

didn't think about it until right now? I could feel a good freak-out building up. I think Carter must have been sensing it too, because he took my hand with his free one and linked our fingers. "I wouldn't do anything to hurt you. Ever."

His words made me feel better, but I still felt stupid for not thinking of birth control before I jumped him. That is not the way I am. I have always been scrupulous about things like that. I looked down at our joined hands and felt a little better. I had someone who honestly cared about me and my wellbeing. That was a first. Well, besides Cheryl, of course. How ironic that the only two people I could recall actually caring about my life were my best friend and her younger brother. Strangely enough, I hadn't been thinking of Carter as Cheryl's little brother. He was his own entity to me now. The past couple of days had allowed me to see him in his own right, and I really liked what I was getting to know. Even without remembering our history together, I could see that we were a good fit.

"Thanks Carter. I'm sorry; my head is all over the place." I left my hand in his for a second more before I withdrew it to finish our task. He didn't say anything but turned back to the dwindling pile of vegetables. Once they were all trimmed and cleaned we washed up and I went back into chef mode.

"Could you chop some garlic?" I asked as I separated the asparagus into freezer bags.

"Yep." He pulled a huge head of garlic from the bowl on the counter and pulled out my favorite knife.

"Do you like cooking?"

"Love it. Plus, it's nice to be able to spend time in the kitchen with you." He smiled at me and I felt my familiar butterfly friends start flapping around in my stomach. *Is he for real?* He seemed to be my perfect mate. It was also nice to realize we were passing the awkwardness of the bedroom and would probably not have to have a "talk" about what happened. Well duh, I guess this isn't the first time we had been together. It was just feeling so new to me that I was expecting to have to go through all the new relationship crap.

My phone rang just as I started to measure the rice. "Will you start heat up some olive oil, Carter?" He nodded and I walked over to my purse. It was my mother.

"Hi Mom."

"Justine, how are you doing today?" She sounded genuinely concerned. It felt nice.

"I'm doing a lot better. I started to remember some things. First thing this..." She didn't even let me finish my sentence.

"Oh good. I knew you would get over it soon. Listen, I've just been invited to Phoenix for the week to stay with my friend Tina, and Sue is out of town visiting her daughter, so I need you to watch Monique for me. I'm driving to the airport tonight, so I could just drop her off on my way. You're at home, right?" What the heck? I didn't even like her cat, she was a spoiled wretch.

"Uh Mom, she doesn't get along with Lucy. She's always chasing her and swatting her." Not to mention how she treats me.

"Well maybe you could keep them separated or something. It's only until Sunday." Was she crazy? That would be a full time job.

"I don't know. I'm not really up to pet sitting

right now. I still don't have my memory back and I don't know how Carter would feel about it." I looked over at him to see him raising his brows at my conversation.

"Well, you're my last resort, Justine, and as my daughter I would think that I would be able to depend on you when I need help." She sounded huffy and I felt defeated, it was just like I felt living with her growing up.

"Fine, you can bring her." I gave in. I couldn't say anything that would change her mind anyway. "What time will you be here?"

"Well, I'm still a little way outside of Austin, so I should be at your house in less than an hour. Bye." *She was almost here.* She hung up before I could say another word. There was no way the trip was *this* last minute. I felt used, a common sensation from my youth.

Geez. No "thank you" or even "please" from my mother. She just assumed I would watch her cat for her no matter the inconvenience to me. Or Lucy and Carter. Why was I such a pushover?

I set my phone down and looked over at Carter. "My mom is dropping off her cat in an hour. She's going to Phoenix for a week."

He walked over to me and touched my bad cheek. His fingers felt cool. "Don't let her get to you. She doesn't deserve to have that kind of power over you." He dropped his hand and smiled. "We'll take her cat to a kennel and board her for the week, she wouldn't know the difference."

I snorted out a half laugh. "I like the way you think." I looked over the kitchen realizing that she was due to arrive at about the time we were going to eat. "Do you mind if we put off making the food until after she's gone? I don't want her ruining our dinner and I really don't want to invite her to eat with us, not that she would since she's on her way to the airport, but still."

"No problem. Nothing's been started yet anyway." I sat down at the island and Carter grabbed a bottle of water out of the refrigerator and sat down beside me. Uh oh. I could feel the "talk" coming on after all.

"You told me you love me."

"Yes."

"Why? I mean, what made you say that? Did you remember?"

"No, not really. It's hard to explain. I was looking at you and I couldn't hold back the words. I could feel that I love you. Do you know what I mean?"

He shook his head. "Are you saying you don't know *why* you love me you just do?"

That was it in a nutshell, but it didn't sound quite right. I didn't know what *would* sound right though, so I just shrugged.

"Do you feel bad about the sex?" Why did he have to ask *that* question? I had tried to put the sex out of my mind for the last half hour, but I had done a pretty poor job of it.

"I don't feel bad; I'm just thinking maybe we should have waited." He just looked at me. "Like you said." I had to add that because he had been right. I *wasn't* ready. But damn, it had felt good.

He nodded to me, but he looked disappointed. I wished I could take the last couple of hours back, to before I demanded a kumquat, but the only way that would happen without a time machine was with amnesia, and I already had that.

"I'm not sorry about it, Carter." I reached out to touch his hand and he turned his over and captured mine before I could move it.

"I'm not sorry, either." We sat there again, not talking but connected. It felt good.

"Do you want a glass of wine?" I figured some wine might loosen us up with the added bonus of immunizing me against my mother's visit.

"That sounds good. Red or white?"

"White. I'll get the glasses." He grabbed a bottle of wine out of the refrigerator while I went over to the cabinet and pulled out two glasses. I looked at the label on the bottle before he opened it. Good choice. I stood there while he opened it and poured us each a healthy glass. I raised my drink to toast.

"To getting my memory back."

We clinked and Carter added, "And to surviving Monique for a week."

I was surprised that he knew the name of my mother's cat. "Do you know Monique?"

"Unfortunately, this isn't the first time she has stayed with us." I raised my brow and he shook his head. "I'll fill you in later."

I nodded and took a sip. I was about to sit back down but Carter put a hand on my lower back and propelled me towards the living room. I sat down on the couch next to Lucy and Carter sat down next to me. It was nice and familiar, like we do this often.

I thought now might be as good time as any to get some basic answers. "Carter, what did we do on Friday? That's when this started. Maybe if I can retrace my steps I'll know why I forgot everything."

"Well, I went to work, so I'm not sure how you

spent the bulk of the day, but I do know that you went grocery shopping. I also know you posted an update about autumn vegetables on your blog because I read it while I was at work. Now that I think about it, you were a little anxious when I got home, but you said everything was fine so I took your words at face value. Do you think something happened while I was at work? I guess that could explain the edginess and the fact that you're blocking something. Maybe you got a call from someone. I'll go get your phone. I can't believe I didn't think of this before." He jumped up and went to the kitchen for my phone.

"Do you mind?" He held up the phone asking permission to snoop through my calls.

"Help yourself; I probably won't remember anything anyway."

He opened up my call log and looked through. "Hmm, nothing that I can see. You called me and Cheryl called you twice." He set the phone on the coffee table and sat back with his wine. "Maybe you should call Cheryl and ask her if she can remember what you talked about on Friday."

That sounded like a good idea, and was just about to tell him so when the doorbell rang and Lucy jumped up barking. Crap. Mom was here with her odious cat. It couldn't have been more than twenty minutes since she had called. I looked over at Carter as I got up and he gave me an unenthusiastic look. I was glad I wasn't the only one feeling miserable about what was sure to be an awful undertaking.

Chapter Sixteen

The doorbell rang again just as I was peeking through the peephole. Mom stood out there looking impatient and bothered and for a split second I wished I could just pretend we weren't here. Unfortunately, I had agreed to cat sit, so there was no getting out of it.

I looked over at Lucy on the couch with Carter. She was still barking but she wasn't at the door. I think she may be psychic. It's like she knew that my mom was out there with Monique.

I opened the door and my mother came breezing in hauling the cat crate and a huge bag. It looked like a diaper bag, but it was obviously stuffed with things I would be required to use with Monique.

"Hi Mom. How was your drive?"

"Hi honey. It was long as usual. I have to hurry if I'm going to make it to the airport on time. Oh, hello Carter." Mom gave a smile as Carter stood up. "Here is her bag of toys and food, and I brought her bed, it's still outside in my car." She gave me a look that said "go out and get it" but Carter jumped in.

"I'll go get the bed, Gloria." He shot out the door

leaving me with my mother.

"Your face looks worse than it did the other day. You need more concealer." I gnashed my teeth to avoid saying anything I might regret. "Okay Justine, I have the list of instructions for her tucked into the bag. The most important thing is to make sure she doesn't get outside."

"You know I have a doggy door, right?"

"Well, you'll just have to keep it closed then, won't you? And please don't let Lucy chase her around the house, she's not as young as she used to be." This woman had balls. She was expecting me to inconvenience my baby so that her cat would be comfortable? Lucy was old too, and she couldn't hold her bladder very long. Was I supposed to take her out every half hour? Carter's idea of boarding Monique was sounding better and better.

She leaned down to unlock the crate and Monique strutted out like she owned the place. Lucy, who was no longer barking, had retreated to the far side of the couch, as if she knew what was coming. "Here you go baby, Justine will take care of you while Mommy's gone. I'll be back soon." She bent down and gave the cat a kiss before straightening up and giving me an awkward hug. "I'll be back on Sunday. Take good care of my baby,"

Why didn't she ever treat me the way she treats her cat? Why did I even care anymore? She was making her way back to the door when Carter came back in carrying a hideous rhinestone bedazzled, zebra-striped cat bed.

"Oh, are you leaving already?" He tried to make his voice sound disappointed but it didn't work. I could hear the relief in every word. I'd be relieved, too, if it weren't for the fact that she was leaving behind a cat that was a real pain in the butt.

"Oh, well, I've got to get to the airport; you know how I hate all this city traffic. I'll see you on Sunday. Bye bye." She walked out the door while we stood there silently. What the fudge just happened here? Gloria was in and out in less than five minutes and she didn't even ask how I was. That sucked. She was my mom even if she was self-centered. I looked over to Carter, still standing next to the couch still holding the cat bed.

"I guess that went better than I was hoping. Faster anyway. She didn't even say thank you." He just looked back at me with sympathy. I looked down at the cat. She was licking her privates on the floor in the middle of my living room. I glanced up and saw Carter staring at her with a look of disgust on his face. I wondered what had happened with Monique before to make him dislike her. Carter loved cats and had even told me he wouldn't mind getting one. Shoot, he loved all animals. Oh. I know that Carter loves cats!

"Carter, you need to thank Monique." He looked at me like I was crazy.

"Why on earth would I need to thank Monique for anything?"

"Because I was looking at you hating on her just now and I thought that she must have done something horrible to you to make you feel like that since you love cats." I looked at him, waiting for him to understand what I was telling him but he didn't. "I remembered you love cats. At least I think I remembered that. You do love them, right?"

"Yeah, I do." He smiled crookedly. "Thanks,

Monique." He put the cat bed down on the floor near the kitchen door before he walked over and pulled the bag off of my shoulder and carried it into the kitchen. I trailed behind him and noticed the dinner ingredients still set out.

"Are you still hungry?" I asked as he put the cat bag on the table.

"I'm starved." He looked around before turning back to me. "Juss, your mom didn't happen to leave some kind of cat box did she?"

"Um, not unless it's stuffed in the bag." I knew it was unlikely that there was some tiny portable cat box in the bag but I walked over and started dumping the contents anyway. "Nope. Nothing here."

"Well, I guess I should run to the store and get something." This was getting worse by the second.

"All right, you do that and I'll get started on dinner."

"No." He practically yelled it at me. He just told me he was starved, so you would think he would appreciate me getting a jump on the food. "Just wait for me, okay? I won't be gone long, I'm sure they have something at the drug store down the street."

"Sure. You do that and I'll finish my wine."

He grabbed his keys and kissed me on the cheek before he left. It made my whole face tingle and I'm sure I was smiling like a loon until I realized I still had to cat proof the house. I was feeling resentful. All this upheaval when I'm not even myself just wasn't fair. I went back to the living room to pick up my wineglass and saw Monique up on the couch. Lucy was nowhere to be seen, so I walked down the hall to my bedroom.

When I looked at the bed I felt a wave of heat

wash through me. I couldn't help but remember what had happened there just a little while ago. When I saw Lucy peek out of the covers and look at me, though, all feelings of lust flew out the window, replaced with my protective motherly instincts. Monique had obviously scared her off of the couch and out of the living room altogether. I walked over and scooped her up, snuggling her under my arm and marching back into the living room to pick up my glass and carry it with me to the kitchen. After I took a big gulp I figured I might as well take Lucy out to do her business since Carter didn't want me starting on the food.

I was still in the backyard watching Lucy sniff around when I heard Carter tap on the door from the inside. He was holding a cat box under one arm and a bag of kitty litter in his hand.

"Do you want it in the laundry room again?" he asked while motioning to the door.

"Oh yeah. I guess that's the best place, out of the way and all that." I let him take care of that while I went to Monique's bag of crap. I pulled out her food and her bowls and fixed her up. The last time I watched her I had to put her dishes up on my buffet table so that Lucy wouldn't eat it; I guess I had to do that again, but I just hated having the cat on my buffet; it seemed so dirty. After I was finished with that I went into the laundry room to see how Carter was doing with the kitty toilet.

I could hear him cussing under his breath when Lucy and I walked in. It made me feel good, like he was a real person, not just the person I had been seeing since yesterday. I mean, someone can't be sweet and helpful all the time, right?

"Hey. Can I start dinner now?" I sure hoped so, I was getting pretty hungry and the wine on an empty stomach was making me feel sappy. I could just imagine a cozy scene like we shared earlier happening every day. Man, that would be awesome. I needed to ask Carter how much time we spent together, usually. For all I know we might do our own thing every evening. I hoped not. I much preferred my mental image of us.

The thought of puttering around the house doing nothing was incredibly appealing. Maybe he was wearing me down, after all. I had to admit that I enjoyed spending time with him. I liked him. I loved him. I still hadn't processed that fully. I pulled myself out of my daydream when I realized he was talking to me.

"I'm sorry. What did you say?"

"I said, "Yes, I'm ready for dinner." Give me a minute to clean up."

"Oh, okay." I turned around and went back to the stove to turn on the pan for the rice while he washed his hands behind me.

"Okay boss, what do you want me to do?" I looked over at the garlic that he hadn't gotten around to chopping and pointed to it. He went to work while I pulled the bottle of wine back out of the refrigerator. He brought his pile of garlic over to the stove and stood next to me. It felt good, like we were a team. I didn't even feel the usual nervousness that attacked me when I was around a good looking man. And seriously, Carter was possibly the hottest guy I had ever actually talked to. Oh, there was the waiter Jeff, at work, but he was gay so it didn't really count.

"Carter, do we spend a lot of time together?"

"Well, I think so. We spend most evenings together, is that what you mean?"

"Yes, but what do we do? Do we hang out around the house or what? I guess I just want to know how we spend our time."

He looked at me and smiled. "Yeah, we pretty much hang around the house. We aren't lame though." I raised my eyebrow at him. It sounded like we might be a *little* bit lame. "Really, we go out to eat and stuff. Sometimes we'll have people over, too. Mostly just Cheryl and Paulo, but still, we're not shut-ins. I think we're pretty cool." *Says the Star Wars geek.* Maybe Carter was cool, but I had never been "cool" in my life. I was slightly bookish in school and then in college I didn't go out much until I met Cheryl. However, if I was able to land a hot guy like Carter, maybe I *was* cool. I suddenly remembered that I have a web show and a cookbook in the works. I *am* cool. I had to keep that in mind. Whatever transformation had taken place in my life in the last two years turned me into someone cool and it was great.

"I wish I could remember." I looked into his eyes and they were full of sadness, but also something else. I turned back to the pan and stirred in what I figured would be the last ladleful of broth. "Do you want to listen to some music?"

"Yeah." He went into the living room and a few seconds later I could hear "*Electric Avenue*" coming through the speakers. I confess a weakness for cheesy Eighties music. When Carter came back in I was singing along and dancing in front of the stove. He just smiled and started doing the Robot. He wasn't even embarrassed. And thinking of cheese, I added a good handful of shaved parmesan to my rice. *Perfect.*

"Time to eat." Carter had grabbed a fresh bottle of wine while I plated the food and slid it across the island.

"Mmm. This is great." Carter gave me a thumbs up.

I tried a bite and had to agree with him. We ate in silence for a few minutes, until my phone rang. I got up to get it out of the living room.

"Let it ring," Carter told me between bites.

"It might be my mom. She probably hasn't left yet." I jogged to grab it but it stopped ringing before I got to it. Elisa again. Maybe Carter knew who this was.

I walked back to my seat with the phone. "Who is Elisa?"

"Just someone I work with. She's glommed on to you and she thinks she's your friend. You don't really like her." He used air quotes around "friend" so I could tell that *he* didn't like her, but she'd already called me twice so we were at least friendly.

"She called yesterday, too. I haven't listened to the voicemail yet." Carter's face froze for a moment but almost instantly smoothed.

"I'm sure it's nothing important." He went back to eating so I put my phone down wondering what his change of facial expression meant. Was he cheating on me? No, that didn't make sense. He was too attentive, and he was trying hard to help me get my memory back. I tried to shrug it off but something about her name was nagging at my brain. We finished the food and I stood up to grab the mousse from the refrigerator.

Carter looked up at me and smiled when I set his down in front of him. I just about melted. All I wanted to give him a kiss, but I couldn't make myself do it. It was still too early. I know we had just had sex a few hours ago, but this was different. Now that my mind wasn't clouded with lust something else was filling it. Tenderness. I just smiled back and sat back down.

My first bite of the chocolate mousse made something short circuit in my mind. Well, it was that or the Pet Shop Boys song that had just started playing. Perhaps it was a combination of both, but I knew immediately what Carter had done.

"This is just like our first date." His eyes widened and I knew I was right. He nodded and grabbed my hand.

"I can't believe it actually worked and that you remembered." He was practically bursting at the seams.

"I can't believe I didn't figure it out sooner. Monopoly? You were pulling out all the stops." I shook my head but left my hand in his.

"I didn't mention the mousse; you did that all by yourself." That's right. I remembered craving it when I was thinking about what to serve with our food.

"Thank you, Carter." I leaned forward at the same time he did. We didn't stop until we were touching noses.

"My pleasure. I'll recreate every day until you remember everything, if you want." A chill went up my spine and I took a breath full of Carter. I touched my lips to his and I tasted the chocolate. I was just about to really get into it when I heard Lucy yelp from the other room. I jerked my head back and we both bolted into the living room. Lucy was cowering in the corner near the bookshelves and Monique was standing in front of her trying to look innocent. I had forgotten she was here.

Carter reached down and picked up Lucy. I checked her for blood but she was unmarked. Lucky for Monique.

"I don't like this cat, Carter."

"Believe me, I don't either." He handed Lucy to me. "Stupid cat ruined our date night."

What? He was going to let the cat defeat him. I. Don't. Think. So.

Chapter Seventeen

"Oh no she didn't," I told Carter as he turned to face off with Monique. "We are going to finish our date." On this point I was standing firm. I was starting to remember and I wasn't going to let my mother's cat derail something good.

"Juss, I have to concentrate right now. This is serious business." He hadn't taken his eyes off of Monique. "Could you please go over there and open her crate for me? I need it to be ready."

He was going to crate her? I frowned on that. My mom was entrusting me with her most precious thing. And, no, the irony that the cat was more precious to her than her own flesh and blood did not escape me.

"Carter, I don't think we should put her in the crate. My mom wouldn't like that." Boy, talk about understatements.

"Babe, you don't know the full situation. This cat doesn't like me."

Did this cat like anyone? "She doesn't like me either, but we can't just keep her locked up."

"Juss, she attacks me at every opportunity. She

draws *blood*. I'm not putting up with her for a week. I'm sorry; I know I should have said something earlier." He's not putting up with her? Excuse me, but wasn't this *my* house? Okay, so I realize he lives here, too, even if I don't fully remember yet, but I wasn't going to have him putting the cat in a small crate for who knows how long.

"I'm sorry, Carter, but I can't let you do that. My mother is counting on me."

"I'm not going to crate her for a week; I'm just going to use it to carry her to the laundry room so that I can shut her in there for tonight. I think we are going to have to get her out of the house."

"Why? I know she's kind of a pain and she doesn't get along with Lucy, but really, she isn't *that* bad."

He just looked at me like I was slow and shook his head. "She's out to get me, Juss. She *attacks* me. Do you understand what I'm saying? She wants to *destroy* me." Where was the sexy and protective Carter from before? I was almost embarrassed for him. She wanted to *destroy* him? Where did he get this stuff?

"Look, she hasn't done anything to you yet. Let's just give her a chance. She might have mellowed since you last saw her." I could tell he didn't want to let it go, but he sighed and backed away from Monique, taking my arm and pulling me away, too.

"Let's just eat our mousse and relax. We have a date to get back to, right? Come on, we'll take them to the couch and watch something on TV, okay?" He nodded and grabbed our dishes since I was still holding Lucy. Carter walked over to the stereo and turned it off with his elbow before coming to sit with me. I made sure Lucy was sandwiched between us before I took back my mousse and I started eating. It really was delicious. Carter turned on the TV then put his feet up on the coffee table.

"Shark Week." He looked over and gave me a grin. Okay, he might be scared of a cat, but his grin could get me every time. Dammit! I just wanted to remember him fully. The snatches I've been getting had all made me feel better, but there was still just a little bit of weirdness there. Even after having mind-blowing sex. Maybe because of the sex, I didn't know anymore. All I was sure of was that Carter and I were together and he was, quite possibly, the most romantic guy ever born. Reenacting our first date was awesome. Even if I had my memory, that would be romantic. Ahh.

I nodded and took another bite. Maybe I should do a web show on mousse. Maybe I already had. I needed to know these kinds of things. That was going to be on my to-do list for tomorrow. Learn how to do my job.

"Carter, have I done a show about mousse yet?"

"No, but for the next series of recipes that would be a good addition."

"What do you mean series? Don't I just do a show and post it?"

"Uh uh. It's more complicated than that. We have to do repeat shots sometimes and then there's the lighting and sound to set up, not to mention the editing involved before it's ready." Wow. It sounded almost like a real TV show, or what I knew about a TV show.

"Who does all of that?" Surely the two of us couldn't do everything.

"Paulo. He brings his stuff over and we try to do at least three segments at a time. It really saves a lot of time that way. He edits them for us, too."

Hmm. This sounded like a professional operation we had going here. I felt a surge of pride. Never in my wildest dreams did I think I would actually be able to do a cooking show, but here I was with a show and a book coming out. This was fantastic.

I settled back into the couch feeling happy. Really happy. Look at me, Justine Taylor, sitting on the couch with an incredibly sexy man who had just rocked my world, eating chocolate and thinking about my awesome career. It really didn't get much better than this. Well, besides the amnesia. But Carter was even helping me take care of that.

I couldn't bask in the glow of happiness long because, out of the corner of my eye, I could see a flash of black and white fur. Monique had climbed up the back of the couch and launched an attack. Carter screamed and threw his cup of mousse into the air as he jumped up with Monique attached to his head.

"Aaaah!" Monique was holding on with her claws and Carter was flailing around trying to peel her off of his scalp. "Help me!"

I was already trying to get to him but it was hard since he was moving around so much. "Hold still!" He paused with his hands covering his eyes and I grabbed Monique by the front legs. Wow, she was really in deep. It took me a moment to pull her off of him.

I had her in my hands and Lucy was barking at all of the frantic activity as Carter lunged for the crate. I shoved her inside before she could turn on me. What the hell had just happened? Carter set the crate down with more force than necessary, but I didn't blame him. There was blood seeping from his hairline. I pulled his head down closer to my eyes and I could see three tiny puncture marks in his scalp.

"She got this side too," he said as he turned his head to show me. I felt like an ass. He said she was after him and I hadn't believed him. Now he was injured and it wouldn't have happened if I would have let him put her in the laundry room.

"I'm so sorry, Carter. I didn't think she would go after you like this." I led him into the kitchen and tore off a paper towel and wet it in the sink. I started dabbing it on his puncture wounds and realized they weren't as bad as I had originally thought. Whew.

"I tried to tell you, she's the devil." He said it with such sincerity that I couldn't stop the smile.

"I'm sorry I didn't believe you. Well, you don't need stitches, anyway, and there's too much hair for using a Band-Aid. We can just keep it clean." I paused and looked over to the cat crate. "We can set her up in the laundry room." I knew we were going to have to board her now. There was no way I would feel comfortable knowing Monique was capable of this kind of behavior. She had never shown me this amount of aggression. She must really hate Carter. He hadn't done anything to her since she got here, but I knew she must have been planning this all along.

When I picked up the crate Monique looked at me as if *she* were the victim. I wasn't going to fall for it. She had hurt my man. Yes, *my* man. I may not remember him fully, but I was claiming him. Even if I didn't already know him I would be falling for him on my own right now. He was great company and he was thoughtful and sensitive, and that's not even considering the sex. That was a whole other issue. I set the crate down in the laundry room and turned to see Carter behind me with her food and water bowls. He set them down as I bent to open the crate.

"Wait. Let me get out of here first." He bolted to the door and shut it behind him and I carefully opened the door of the crate half expecting her to launch herself at me, but she sauntered out and went to her food bowl. If I hadn't just seen it for myself, I wouldn't have believed she could be so vicious. She had betrayed me by attacking Carter after I had gone to bat for her to keep her from being locked up. I was totally on Carter's side and I wasn't ashamed. By the time I made it back to the kitchen Carter was wetting a dish rag.

"I spilled my mousse," he said as he walked back to the living room. A long brown stripe was splashed across the floor. Luckily the glass hadn't broken; it rested on the floor next to the mess.

"At least it didn't get on the rug," He just looked up and kept wiping. I could see his wounds were still oozing so I held out my hand. "Here, let me." I pulled him up before taking the rag from him. "You should probably go clean your head up."

He looked down at me and my heart started thumping. I wanted him to kiss me in the worst way but he just smiled and turned toward the bathroom. I looked down at the mess on the floor and sighed. Fucking Monique.

Chapter Eighteen

I looked down at the mousse covered rag and went to wash it out in the sink, deciding to use paper towels to finish the cleanup. Remorse was eating at me. It was my fault Carter was in the bathroom cleaning his injuries right now. If only I would have listened to him.

What now? I wanted to go and check on him but what if he was angry? I was still feeling out of my depth, but I had to make sure he was okay.

I could hear Monique screwing around in the laundry room. She was probably tearing something apart in an act of revenge, but I wasn't about to go check. After witnessing her treatment of Carter, I wasn't completely confident that she wouldn't attack me, as well. I trudged to the bathroom to see what was up with Carter's head. He had the door shut so I gave it a light tap.

"Are you all right?" He didn't answer but he opened the door. I could see the claw marks standing out against his skin and tiny droplets of blood were still coming out of the punctures. He had a washcloth pressed to the other side of his head. I met his eyes in the mirror.

"I'm sorry. I honestly didn't realize she would go lion on wildebeest with you, at least not unprovoked."

"This isn't the first time she's savaged me, Justine." He pointed to a thin, pale scar on his forearm. "This is what she gave me last time she was here." I looked closely at his arm. It was really a magnificent arm, but I couldn't let myself get distracted.

"Why didn't you say something when Mom called?" I mean geez, if I had been fully informed of the danger I would have at least listened to him about putting her in the laundry room.

"It was too late after you got off of the phone, and to be honest, I thought some of the trauma from her last visit might have come back to you." I looked at him in confusion. "Does diarrhea ring a bell?" He waited expectantly for an answer.

Diarrhea? Did the stress of cat watching give me diarrhea? Ewww. If it did I certainly didn't feel comfortable talking about it with Carter. That was too personal even if we were living together. He must have gathered that I wasn't up for talking about my bodily functions right then because he put me out of my misery.

"The *cat* had diarrhea and she didn't limit it to the cat box." *Oh my god, gross.* "She really did a number on the couch and the rug in the bedroom." Worse and worse. What good was this cat anyway?

I didn't have anything left. "Sorry." I was suddenly enraged at my mother. Surely I would have told her what had happened after the last time she left Monique here. She had obviously either used the amnesia to her own benefit or she really didn't care how badly she was putting us out. I was leaning toward the latter. She was selfish enough not to put a bit of thought into how much this was inconveniencing us. No, this went beyond inconvenience. She was putting us in physical danger. What sort of a mother would do that to her only child?

"She must have known all that, right?" He nodded. "Why would she bring her back here?"

"I guess she was hard up for a cat sitter."

"She really doesn't care, does she?"

"I do." Carter reached over with his free hand and pulled me into a hug. I was embarrassed by Gloria's lack of maternal love. I knew Carter couldn't even fathom how it felt; Sharon showered affection on Cheryl and Carter. She went out of her way to make sure they knew they were loved. Cheryl was always receiving care packages from Sharon when we were roomies, even though we lived in the same city. Family dinners at their home, while usually unpalatable, were warm and wonderful. Gloria's...not so much, although things were a little better since she married Bill. He was pretty cool, and I think she tried to put on a front for him. Oh, but she said she divorced Bill. That was just another mark against her in my book.

I let myself stand in his arms, absorbing his pity like a sponge. I knew it was weak since I have had almost thirty years to get used it, but, as always, it hurt. I let him comfort me for a moment more before I remembered he was bleeding from the head.

"Sorry. I came in here to see if I could do

anything for you and you end up making me feel better."

"Stop apologizing, it's done, but I'm calling a kennel first thing tomorrow." He spoke decisively. He wasn't going to take no for an answer and I found that highly arousing.

"Absolutely." I gave in on the kennel without a second thought. Who cares if Gloria (I decided she didn't deserve the title of mom anymore) didn't want to board her *baby*? Not me, that was for sure. "Now, let me see the damage." I stepped back from him and took his head in my hands.

It was ugly and the sight of blood usually made me feel sick, but knowing that I was partly responsible for the damage seemed to hold off the nausea. I felt strong in the manner of a WWII nurse treating soldiers under fire. I just did what had to be done.

"I should put some antibiotic on it," I told him knowledgeably. I went to the cabinet and pulled out the first aid kit. I found some in both cream form and spray so I pulled out the spray figuring it would give lots of coverage without me actually having to touch the blood and cuts.

I held the can near his temple and pushed the button. After a second a weird stream of medicine came spurting out, punctuated by big droplets of white. *Hmm, the nozzle must be clogged.* I was about to turn the can so that I could examine it more closely but Carter grabbed it out of my hand and set it on the counter. He shook his head at the gooey mess on the side of his face and used the wash cloth to wipe it off.

"I'll just use the cream." He grabbed the tube out

of the box and started smearing it on his lacerations as I stood there feeling superfluous. So much for my nursing fantasy; he was obviously fine without my help. I turned to leave the bathroom but he stopped me. "Don't leave. I like you in here tending my wounds. I don't think I've ever had a prettier nurse."

Omigod. It's like he read my mind. I couldn't help the smile that bloomed across my face at his words. He always knew just what to say to make me feel better. I knew instantly that I was recalling this from some time in my hazy past, but nothing in particular stood out, just the knowledge that it was true. It kind of freaked me out, this half remembering, and I searched for an escape. The kitchen was still filthy and I couldn't stand the thought of leaving it like that so I figured now was a good time to leave Carter to his own devices and get my own head together.

"I'm going to go take care of the dishes. You can finish up in here without me," I whispered as I fled. It was a relief to be out of Carter's orbit. He still had the ability to get me flustered. I wondered if I usually reacted like that or if I had gotten used to being around him. I assumed everything was okay since I couldn't imagine inviting him to live with me if I felt even the slightest bit uncomfortable around him, but who knows? Maybe he dazzled me or something.

I cleaned the kitchen while thinking of various scenarios under which I would have asked him to move in. Was it a weak moment after sex? That was a possibility now that I had experienced some of his sexual prowess for myself, but still, that didn't seem like me. Maybe he was hard up for money and needed a roommate so I generously offered him my home. Hmm, that was unlikely. Cheryl got a pretty big inheritance when her grandma died so I figured Carter did too. Maybe I just loved him so much I couldn't stand for him to be too far away from me. While that made me seem a bit needy, it still felt nice.

Before I knew it the kitchen was spotless and I was standing there with nothing to do. Lucy had been hovering around my feet since her own encounter with Monique so I picked her up and carried her with me into the living room. Carter wasn't out there like I was expecting. I poked my head into the bathroom and office which were both empty, and when I opened the door to the bedroom he was standing in front of my night table with his back to me.

"All better?" I asked as I walked into the room. He spun around and I felt myself go hot and cold in one horrifyingly humiliating second. Clutched in his hand was a huge, lifelike penis.

Chapter Nineteen

Holy crap. He found my vibrator. I could feel the blood rushing to my face. Would my humiliations never abate? But wait. I didn't recognize that monstrosity as belonging to me. *Oh my god.* Had I just caught Carter with *his* vibrator? My face got even hotter than I believed possible. I didn't know what to do, but I couldn't look away. I was enthralled by the sight of that huge penis in his hands. Whoa. I shook my head.

"I'm sorry. I didn't mean to interrupt." I started backing out of the room while covering Lucy's eyes with my hand. She *so* didn't need to see this.

"Wait. Juss don't go; it's not what you think." Well, he *would* say that wouldn't he?

"Hey, I'm no one to judge you. Honestly. I'm open minded." I kept backing out until I was in the hallway then I turned around and practically ran back to the kitchen. I needed a minute to absorb what I had just seen but I didn't get it. Carter was two steps behind me still carrying the vibrator in his hands. Well, maybe it was just a dildo; I couldn't tell from this angle.

"This isn't mine." He thrust it in my face and I couldn't help but admire the impressive size of it. "This is Vlad, don't you remember?" He named his fake penis? I thought only I did that. I shook my head at him. I think I would recognize my own special friend.

"Really, Carter, it's okay." I was trying to wrap my head around this latest development but it was just too much.

"Vlad the Impaler?" he questioned me again. Wait. Now that he said it again, that name did seem slightly familiar. "We have a lot of fun with him. Well, you do, but me too because we incorporate it into our sex, but it's for you." His eyes were imploring me to believe him. He seemed to be telling me the truth, but what the fuck was he doing messing with it?

I held up my hand. "Stop. I need a second here." If it was indeed mine, and I guess that really made more sense, the embarrassment was all on me.

"Why were you playing around with it?" That was a question I needed answered immediately.

"It's not like I was stroking it." He sounded exasperated. "I had just picked it up when I was in the sex drawer looking for the remote for the DVD player."

"The sex drawer? Uh uh. I keep my *things* in a box under the bed." I told him piously.

"Babe, we have a sex drawer. Come with me." He took my hand and pulled me and Lucy along with him and back to the bedroom. I wanted to protest but I had to admit to curiosity. The drawer was still open and he pointed down before helpfully turning on the lamp right above it.

Holy moly. I had been right earlier in thinking we may be a little kinky. I recognized "Steve" sitting in the drawer beside several new items. I must have really broken out of my shell. I couldn't imagine leaving all these items out where anyone could find them. I reached out and picked up a bottle. Strawberry flavored lube. Interesting.

Carter put the vibrator back in the drawer and shut it so I decided to give him a break, even though I was cringing inside. "Okay, I believe it's mine. Sorry, you just caught me off guard, that's all."

"Well, obviously you caught *me* off guard." He wanted to laugh it off and I was just cowardly enough to let him. This was just one thing too much at the end of a long and stressful day.

"So, um, did you want to watch some TV?" I asked, remembering the reason I came back here in the first place.

"That would be great. I was just thinking that we could watch a movie back here where it's more comfortable and farther away from the cat." I winced as I was reminded of what had just happened. I looked over the bed which was all smooth and straightened then back to Carter.

I set Lucy down on the bed and walked over to the TV. I could see a movie propped next to the DVD player, *50 First Dates*. I liked this movie, and I really needed some comedy in my life right about now. I turned back to Carter. "This is kind of weird." He looked at me questioningly. "Just everything. You, me, my amnesia, the cat, the vibrator. Everything." I made a sweeping motion with my hand as if to encompass the whole room. I could have made a longer list that included much more, but I figured he could get idea.

"You're right. I've been so set on getting you to remember that I didn't realize I might be pushing you too hard. We can just sit and watch a movie and relax for the rest of the night, all right?" He had walked over to me as he talked and so he was standing just inches away from me right now. I was getting those same overwhelming feelings again but this time I welcomed them. I needed something steady to anchor to. My life had become a freakish situation comedy. I reached out and grabbed his hand and he gave me a squeeze. "Come on, you relax and I'll take care of everything else."

Ahh, just the words I needed to hear. I wanted to let someone else take care of everything for me, if only for a few hours. I needed the mental break.

"That sounds wonderful. Do you mind if I take a bath first? I really need to unwind." Baths were my little escape in my day and always had been. The first house I had looked at in my price range had only had a shower so I had immediately crossed it off my list. I had to have my baths.

"Yeah, you go ahead and take as long as you need. I've got some things I need to do anyway." He paused. "So I guess I should probably post that you're sick and won't be updating for a bit?" He was asking me? He knew way more than I did about that.

"Sure, do what needs to be done. I'm obviously worthless with that right now." I shrugged my shoulders. What was one more thing added to the list today? I went over to my side of the dresser and pulled out some panties and a pair of pajamas, glad that I had upgraded my nightwear in the past two years. Carter had left the room when I started digging for my clothes so I took the opportunity to walk back over to the "sex drawer" and investigate further.

I pawed around at first, afraid to touch anything, but I had to admit, if only to myself, I was impressed. I was finally in one of those couples. The kind that was adventurous and still sweet. Yay me! I moved around the items until I could see everything in the back. There was a remote back there. Hmm, I guess Carter was telling me the truth. I pulled it out and noticed something else. What the...? I pulled out a headband with buns made of fake hair on each side. Princess Leia buns. I got a mental picture of Carter in nothing but a light saber belt. Holy Shit. My face started flaming again. This was too much for even the new me. I hastily shut the drawer and put the remote on top of the table before scurrying to the bathroom and shutting myself in.

I had so many things to think about that I didn't know where to start. I turned on the water and poured in some of my bath crystals. I had remembered a few important things today, and I was incredibly thankful for that, but I was still mostly blank. I could acknowledge, however, that everything I *had* remembered had to do with Carter. He was the key.

I stripped out of my clothes and stepped into the water while it was filling. I loved the water pouring over my feet, and I have always vowed that when I get enough money for luxuries I was going to get a tub with jets. I smiled when I remembered my bank account and the fact that Carter told me I'd be getting a big advance from my cookbook. I made the decision right then that a whirlpool tub was going to be the first thing I bought.

I relaxed back in the hot water and closed my eyes. What a day. I needed a mental break but my mind wouldn't let me have it. The images of the day kept swirling around in my head. The market, the cat, memories flashing back, my mother, the sex. Whew the sex. I let my mind stick on that subject for a while, replaying the event and the time leading up to it. I could safely say that I wanted Carter even without any memories of our relationship. He was just ...awesome. I would have been attracted to him if I had just met him on the street, but once you add in all of his tremendous attributes, who wouldn't find him appealing?

I leaned forward and turned off the water when it got within a half inch of the rim. I let my mind settle back on Carter. He was different than I remembered him, more attentive as well as assertive. It was a strange mix but I liked it. I also liked that he was here for me when I needed him. I knew Cheryl would have taken me under her wing in a heartbeat, but somehow it was just easier with Carter.

I soaked in the tub for a while until I realized that I needed to be out there with Carter. He was going to be the reason I would get my memory back, I just knew it.

I hit the drain and stood up. I couldn't get out of the tub fast enough. I thought about what Carter and I had been talking about before my mother had shown up. We were going to get to the bottom of what happened on Friday. I hurriedly dried off and threw on my pajamas. I couldn't wait to be back in the same room with him.

I hardly stopped to analyze my feelings as I

turned and looked out the hallway. Where was he? I couldn't hear a TV on from the living room or the bedroom so I went into the office. He wasn't there but the computer was still on.

I walked back out to the kitchen where I was greeted by the smell of popcorn. Carter was holding my phone and frowning.

"What's wrong?"

"Not a thing." He deliberately pasted a smile on his face while he set it on the counter. "Did you have a nice bath?"

I let him change the subject because if it was something bad I really didn't want to know. Not tonight, anyway. I wanted the rest of the night to go smoothly.

"It was great." What else was there to say really? I walked over to him and practically nudged up against him. "Do you want any help?"

"Got it covered." He motioned to the counter behind him where he already had some glasses filled with iced tea. He also had a bag of Hershey Kisses sitting there. I could go through a whole bag of kisses during a movie. I ate those like other people ate popcorn. My heart warmed as I realized he knew that much about me.

The microwave beeped and Carter pulled out the popcorn and poured it into a bowl.

"Shall we?" he asked as he scooped up the bowl in one hand and the kisses in another.

I just nodded and grabbed the glasses before trailing him into the bedroom. He walked to one side of the bed and I went to my side, the side next to the "sex drawer." Just being in here was making me think about what was inside it and I was feeling my cheeks warming. I set the drinks down on the table and noticed the remote control I had found in the drawer a few minutes ago.

"Here." I handed him the remote and sat down on the bed.

"Where was it?"

"Uh, it must have fallen behind the table." I certainly wasn't going to admit where I found it. He just looked at me and raised an eyebrow. I tried braving it, but my stupid blush made it impossible. "Oh shut up."

He chuckled and went over to put the movie on. I settled on the bed and watched while he got everything ready. He looked so big and firm and I couldn't help but notice the way the muscles on his back rippled when he moved. He was like my perfect man ideal. Well, besides the fact that he was younger, but to be honest, that was a selling point.

"Did we watch this on our first date or something?" Maybe he was still trying to get me to remember it, but this didn't seem familiar.

"No, but I didn't feel like watching cable on the couch."

"Oh." I settled back on the pillows and Carter flipped on the lamp beside him while the menu came up. He wasn't being as laid-back as he had been before my bath and was making me feel slightly uneasy. I wondered what might have happened in the half hour I was in the bathroom but I no longer felt comfortable asking him.

The movie started and I handed him his drink which he took without saying anything or even looking at me. What the heck was going on? This was like a complete one-eighty from before. I sat there stewing as the movie started. I started unwrapping kisses and shoving them into my mouth without really thinking. Great, now I was going to have a huge ass on top of everything else. Finally, about twenty silent minutes into the movie I couldn't take it anymore.

Chapter Twenty

"What the hell is your problem, Carter?" I sounded bitchy but by this time I really didn't care.

"*I* don't have a problem."

"What's that supposed to mean? I'm not the one who's been sitting here silent and broody for the last half hour. I'm not the one who is ignoring the person sitting beside me."

He didn't bother to answer me and I don't know why, but it made me jumpy. "Hey, I'm talking to you." He didn't say anything before getting up off of the bed and walking toward the door.

"Where are you going?" I couldn't believe he was going to walk out and basically give me the cold-shoulder.

"I need a drink." He didn't turn around and I looked over to his bedside table where I noticed his glass still full. He was obviously leaving the room because of me, but I didn't have the faintest idea of what I could possibly have done to upset him. I had just been thinking about how good I felt around him and how I wanted to spend more time with him. Was I destined to be perennially backwards in this relationship? Was this some kind of curse? Just a couple of days ago I had been freaked out that he and I were together and would have been happy to be by myself while he wanted to be with me, and right now I want to spend time with him and he was avoiding me. It didn't seem fair. Things were different now and my life was supposed to *work*.

I thought about getting up and following Carter to wherever he had gone but I still had my pride. I wasn't going to chase him down when he wanted to be away from me. Still, I might have read things wrong. It certainly wouldn't be the first time I had made an assumption that turned out to be completely false. His attitude might not have anything to do with me at all. I was wavering but I didn't want to look desperate.

I suddenly remembered Monique in the laundry room. It had been a while since I shut her in there. I should probably go check to see that she wasn't wreaking any havoc on my clothes. It was a lame excuse, but it was all I could come up with on short notice and I was feeling emotionally vulnerable.

I jumped up before I could change my mind and walked into the hallway. I could see that the office light was off so I continued to the bathroom. The door was shut but the light was on. Maybe he was in there. I didn't hear anything and after a few seconds I realized how sick I was standing outside the bathroom door and listening for goodness knows what. I quickly moved on and into the dim kitchen. The only light was coming from the small fixture over the sink. I guess he *was* in the bathroom.

Monique wasn't making the racket she had been, so I felt relatively safe opening the door and poking my head in. I didn't see her but I saw an overturned basket of clothes. I didn't know if they had been clean before, but I knew they were dirty now. I detected the horrible odor of cat pee and the wet spots on whatever blue piece of clothing that was lying on top of the pile seemed to corroborate my thoughts on what she had been up to.

I stepped farther into the room to locate the animal I could now verify was vicious as well as just plain gross, and she cemented her evilness by leaping out from behind the door and slicing my bare foot with her claw.

"Aaaaaiiiiiiigh!" The scream that escaped me was only partially from the pain. Most of it was fear and surprise.

Within seconds the back door flew open and for the second time in two days, Carter charged into the room looking for whatever had put me in peril. I crashed into him as I jerked back to escape.

"What happened?" he asked as he grabbed the door handle and pulled it closed, keeping Monique contained.

"That fucking cat attacked me!" I normally didn't like to use the f-word, but my heart was pounding from fright and my foot was in searing pain. I kicked my foot out in front of me to get a better look at the damage but I misjudged the distance to the wall and my big toe connected with a loud thud.

"Ugh. Oh my god." I reached down to grab my foot and started hopping on my left leg. "Ouch, ouch, ouch." I was trying to pant through my pain using the Lamaze trick I had mastered over the years of being clumsy but it wasn't helping. I felt Carter's hands on my upper arms where he grabbed on to steady me.

"Hang on. Let's go into the kitchen where we can get some better light." He held on to me as he walked us both to the kitchen and flipped on the overhead lights. I plopped down on my usual stool and swung my foot up onto the other one. He stood over me and surveyed the damage. It didn't escape my notice that even though he was bothered by something that I may or may not have done, he was taking the time to care for my injury. He was too good for regular people.

"How bad is it?" I hated the sight of blood and my own made me sickest of all. From the amount of burning I was imagining the row of stitches I would be subjected to shortly. Luckily, I knew my toe was just stubbed, I had broken a toe before and the pain was entirely different.

"She didn't break the skin."

"*What?*" There was no way I could be feeling like this with no open wound. It didn't seem possible. I turned my foot so that I could see for myself and realized that Carter was right. There wasn't even one drop of blood. I was relieved but incredulous. That much pain and her claws hadn't even broken the surface? Poor Carter must be in agony with the damage to his head.

I looked up to see him giving me the "I told you she was deadly" look. I managed to refrain from physically rolling my eyes at him, but that didn't stop me from doing it mentally.

"How's your head?" I wasn't sure if he was talking to me yet so I figured I would play it safe and ask after his health.

"Okay. How's yours?" For a moment I had forgotten that I had a head injury.

I gave him a smile. "I'm feeling pretty good." Well, I had been up until he became miffed at me for some reason. "Are you talking to me now?" He looked at me with a mixture of sadness and anger, or maybe it was hurt. I wasn't sure because I didn't know the cause. I frantically tried to remember what I could have done to hurt his feelings. I had nothing. Was this about the cat? Was he angry that I gave in to my mother? But no, he was still okay before I went to take my bath, and he was weird when I came out. Maybe this wasn't about me after all. I felt a faint hint of relief.

"I was never *not* talking to you."

"Yes, I could tell because of all the scintillating conversation since I've gotten out of the tub." I didn't resort to sarcasm very often, either. What was happening to me? I was becoming totally unrecognizable to myself. My head started to hurt. Great, all I needed now was a headache.

He just shook his head and stood there. I took a moment to really look at him. He looked tired. And beaten down. He hadn't looked like that earlier and I was sure of that.

"Damn it, Carter. What is wrong? Just tell me. What did I do?"

He looked at me for about ten seconds without saying anything. I wasn't entirely sure if he planned to answer me at all, but then he spoke, breaking the awkward silence.

"What's so wrong with me?" Huh?

"What do you mean?" I knew I must look completely baffled because I didn't know what he could possibly be talking about.

"What is wrong with me?" He spoke the words

slower and stronger this time. I felt I was still missing something. I shook my head mutely. I didn't know what he was looking for so I wasn't saying anything.

He was too good looking maybe, but I was pretty sure he was expecting me to say something else. He was probably too nice, but maybe that was just with me while I was recuperating. Geez, I couldn't think of anything *really* wrong with him at all. Well, the Star Wars room was a little weird, but we're obviously both a little freaky. Was this some kind of trick question?

"Do you still have a problem with my age?"

Where was he pulling this out of? I shook my head again. I hadn't given his age much of a thought today besides the few minutes when Cheryl had been here. Wait a minute, he was asking me if *I* had a problem? So this *was* about me or something I had said. But what? I hadn't said a thing about having a problem with him. As far as I was concerned the day had only gotten better.

"*What did I do?* If you are upset about something spill it, I'm not going to play a guessing game with you." Now I was feeling defensive. I got mean when I was on the defense, kind of like a coyote in a trap.

"I just got off of the phone with Elisa. Now everything is clear to me. I am *never* going to be what..." I could see that he was deciding whether to tell me whatever it was that had him aggrieved. He opted to keep me in the dark. "Nothing. It's nothing. Forget it. Let's go finish the movie."

"Are you for real? Do you think I'm just going to go watch TV with you without you telling me what's happened? This is Cheryl's rehearsal dinner all over.

When are you going to understand that you don't have to keep things from me? I'm a big girl. I can handle a little anger, especially if I deserve it."

"You remember Cheryl's rehearsal dinner?"

"Well duh, you spent the whole time ignoring me because you were mad that I was joking about being your sugar mama. You didn't even bother to tell me why you were angry until we were at home. It's pretty messed up when your own mother calls you an ass. It almost ruined Cheryl's party. You might be a mind reader but I'm not, Carter. You have to tell me what's bothering you or how can I fix it?" I suddenly realized that I did indeed remember the party as well as the whole night that followed. It hadn't been our first fight, but it had been our biggest. He had been extremely hurt believing I didn't take him seriously.

"Oh. Yeah, I remember." After everything that had transpired today, another memory popping into my head was feeling old-hat. I gave him a small smile but he didn't return it. "What? Does this have something to do with Cheryl's party?"

"No. It doesn't have anything to do with anything. I'm sorry; this is just an off night for me." Now he pasted on a half smile and reached out a hand to me. It was like he suddenly got over whatever was bothering him and he was his old self. I was still a few paces behind him.

"Dang it. You just got me all riled up and now you're fine? How are you able to go from hot to cold in an instant? How can we spend the rest of our lives together when you can't even tell me what's bothering you at any given time? This is my life, too. Don't bottle things up. Don't be such a *man*." Whoa. Did I just say all that? I could suddenly remember having this same conversation with him rehearsal dinner night, but that night I hadn't mentioned spending the rest of our lives together. I was remembering some other things as well, and suddenly, like a plug popping out of a dam, memories started flooding back. The most important thing that popped into my mind though, was a very enlightening conversation I had had. I also remembered who Elisa was.

"Sorry, but I *am* a man. You're right though, I'll try to be more open." He must have seen a change on my face because he started looking at me with concerned eyes. "What is it?"

I only answered with a shake of my head. I wasn't ready to process what my mind just gave me back. I was pretty sure I had just had my breakthrough and instead of feeling relief, all I felt was dismay.

Chapter Twenty One

My mind was flooded with everything I'd been trying so hard to remember. It was different than I'd thought it would be. I wasn't having a "bingo" moment; it was more like dozing off and being woken in a strange place and not knowing where you were. In those first few seconds everything comes back to you and you lose that sense of confusion.

Carter was still looking at me strangely. Oh my god. My poor, sweet Carter. I reached over and grabbed him into a hug. It felt good to hold onto him knowing how important he was to me. I didn't realize how empty I had felt until this moment. How the hell could I have forgotten *Carter*?

I was about to share my wonderful news with him, but when I pulled back to speak, I remembered something else. I remembered the big hunk of emerald surrounded by diamonds that I found in Carter's underwear drawer. Holy smokes! How the heck could I have forgotten that gorgeous, panic inducing ring? Suddenly the events of Friday came back to me as clear as a bell. Cheryl roping me into a shopping trip, Elisa calling and telling me that Carter was going to propose, then tearing up the house looking for the ring. *Oh. My. God.*

I pressed my face back against Carter; I suddenly didn't want to tell him I remembered everything. He was sure to quiz me on Friday and I didn't know what to tell him. If I told him the truth he would be both upset and disappointed by both the ruined surprise and my reaction to it. Plus, that meant he would ask me to marry him very soon.

And I did I want to spend the rest of my life with him. There really was no question in my mind that he was it for me. The problem was marriage itself. I had no idea what the hell a good marriage looked like. I had grown up in a home in which marriage wasn't something that I was exposed to. I really hadn't had that many more examples of wedded bliss from my friends' families either. My childhood best friend Allison was shuttled between her mother and father, so spending the night at her house didn't give me the feeling of family. When Gloria and I moved from Houston to Waco when I was fifteen, my best friend Jennifer was the product of a "broken" home as well. I hadn't really spent any time around a normal married couple until college, joining Cheryl for dinners and the occasional beach vacation with Sharon and Robert. And Carter.

My heart started pounding when I realized what he would be expecting from marriage. Except for being a terrible cook, Sharon seemed like Martha Stewart's long lost twin. Carter grew up in a stable and stylish home and I grew up with a strangely selfish hippie wannabe. I was no Sharon—I knew I never could be. All my distress started building back up; I knew I wasn't equipped for a life like that.

Carter grabbed my shoulders and pulled me off of his chest.

"What's the matter? Your heart is pounding like a rabbit. Jesus, you're white as a sheet. Take a breath and tell me what's wrong with you."

I pulled air into my lungs and forced my face into a smile. My heart was still beating like I was on a treadmill, but I managed to pull my thoughts together. I was conflicted on my next actions. I wanted to tell Carter the truth, at least that way he could stop worrying about me, but I needed time. I made a split second decision to keep this new development to myself. It was the only thing I could think to do.

"Nothing's the matter. It's just been a long day and I started feeling a panic attack coming on, but I'm okay now. Thanks." I fell back on my old foe, the panic attack. I had really been doing better lately; I hadn't had one in forever. Well, except for the hospital, but that was a special circumstance. I felt guilty about my lie when Carter started rubbing slow circles on my upper back.

"It'll be okay, love. Just breathe, I'm here with you. Do you need a cool cloth?" I closed my eyes and let him pull me close in a comforting hug. I was evil and didn't deserve his nurturing treatment. What kind of cow would keep something *this* big from the most important person in her life?

"I'm fine now. Really." I took one last deep sniff of his chest before I pulled back again. My head felt heavy and my temples were throbbing. Oh right, I had a huge knot on my skull. "I'm just going to take some aspririn." I walked a few steps to the cabinet where we kept the medicines and pulled out the bottle of tablets. When I lined up the arrows and popped the top off the pills shot out of the bottle and all over the counter and the floor. "Dang it."

I bent down and started to sweep the pills together with my hand before Carter squatted down beside me, stilling my fingers with his own.

"Stop and tell me what's wrong. Please." He was looking at me imploringly, a look that got me every time. I wanted to spill my guts and rush him like a football player. I felt like I'd just gotten my life back and I wanted to celebrate, but the need to hide out from reality just a little bit longer was too strong to deny. I had to process everything that was swimming in my brain.

"I promise I'm okay. I just have a headache and my foot still stings. Do you mind if I go lie down for a little while?" I could see that he wanted to say something else but he took his hand back and started picking up the dropped pills.

"Sure. You go on and I'll be in a bit. No, I'll get these," he told me when I went to gather a loose pain killer.

I nodded and stood up, grabbing two aspirin off of the counter as I went. I knew what I needed to do. I walked around Carter, still on the floor, and flipped off the door to the laundry room as I passed. Fucking Monique. I couldn't believe Gloria. She totally used my amnesia against me earlier. I told her after the last time that I wouldn't cat sit for her ever again. I was going to let Carter take her to a kennel first thing tomorrow. I didn't even feel a drop of remorse about it, either.

I walked down the hallway quickly; I had to do this before Carter was finished in the kitchen. I made it to the bedroom and quietly closed the door before bolting over to the dresser. I jerked out Carter's underwear drawer and ran my hand along the bottom. Nothing. I pulled the drawer out further and lifted up some stacked boxers. Still nothing. What the hell? I knew it had been right there in the corner. I had put it back carefully in exactly the same place I found it. I shoved the drawer closed and opened his sock drawer right underneath. Nada.

Where was it? This was horrible. Had he changed his mind? The thought didn't comfort me like I was expecting. Instead, it made my stomach drop. What if he did? It wasn't unheard of. My head started spinning as I slid the drawer shut quietly. I didn't realize how much I wanted him to want me that way. Even though I was scared, it was nice to know he loved me that much. It was flattering, too. Nobody had ever loved me that much in my *life*. Not even Gloria. I loved the fact that he adored me. It was a darn good feeling and one that I reciprocated fully. I had never loved anyone as much as Carter, not even Cheryl, and that was saying something.

I felt strangled, like I couldn't breathe. What if he didn't want to marry me anymore? Suddenly the idea of being married to him seemed like the most wonderful thing in the world and the fact that it might not happen was completely unacceptable. I tried to think of where else it could be, and I ran to his bedside table. I rummaged through the contents trying in vain to find the ring, but after a few seconds I knew it was fruitless. My shoulders sagged in defeat and I closed my eyes in an effort to calm myself. This wasn't getting me anywhere. I needed to stop and *think*.

While I sat there I thought back to Elisa's call the other day. She told me Carter's secret and ruined what could possibly have been the most wonderful night of both of our lives. What a bitch move. Why would she have done it? I couldn't wrap my mind around that. When she was telling me, she made it sound like she was doing me a favor and letting me in on a wonderful secret, but what a fucking nerve. How *dare* she ruin that for me? I made a promise to never invite her back to my house. I hated her. Carter was right. She was an evil bitch. How could I have not seen that before?

This was all her fault. She's the reason I got all worked up in the first place, digging around and invading Carter's privacy and then freaking out when I found what I had been searching for. It was her fault I had time to freak out in the first place. I probably would have just told Carter yes and saved myself all this angst. That bitch is most likely the reason I had amnesia too! I was outraged. What if my amnesia made Carter decide that I was too much trouble? *Oh my god.* She had ruined my life.

I threw myself down on the bed and groaned. My whole life was in shambles. I thought back to the past couple of days. I had run from Carter's kiss yesterday, and then later I had practically attacked him. I made him sleep on the couch last night and then jumped him after we played Monopoly. Oh, and let's not forget the way I treated him when I woke up in the hospital. I basically told him there was no way I'd ever be in a relationship with him. He probably thought I was crazy. Hell, I *was* crazy; the only difference was that now *he* knew it, too.

I was flat out wallowing in misery when I had an

inspiration. Maybe he hid it in the bathroom. I jumped up and ran to the bathroom, pulling open all of the drawers. I even looked in the cabinet I kept my tampons in. I searched through the towels and the sheets and I was shoving lotion bottles aside when Carter interrupted my search.

"What's going on?" I froze. Crap. I turned around slowly looking at the trail of mess I had left in my wake. The drawers were open and there were random items strewn haphazardly over the countertops. The towels looked as if Lucy had been trying to make a nest in there. Had I lost my mind? I didn't even remember wrecking everything in my hunt.

"Where is it?" I demanded

"Where is what?"

"My ring?"

"I guess in your jewelry box."

"Why would you put it in my jewelry box?" That didn't even make sense, but I shot out of the door past him and went to my jewelry box. I pulled open the lid almost reverently, this was the moment. I didn't realize I was holding my breath until I released it with a whoosh. It wasn't there. Disappointment crashed through me. I looked up at the doorway where Carter was standing and watching me. "It's not here."

"Which ring are you looking for? It might be in the bowl on the kitchen windowsill." I looked at him in confusion. He wasn't getting it.

"My *engagement* ring, Carter. Where is it?"

Chapter Twenty Two

"What?" Carter's voice was weak and his face was a mask of horror and surprise. It took me a minute to realize that I had just demanded an engagement ring that I had not been offered yet. My own face got hot with mortification. *What had possessed me to ask him that?* I was most probably never going to get it now. I floundered for a second unable to think of anything to say that would extricate me from the quicksand of my stupidity. When was I ever going to learn to turn on my verbal filter?

"Oh, Carter. I'm so sorry." I had pulled my hand over my mouth, something I should have done about twelve seconds ago.

"Juss, did you remember something?" He sounded so hopeful that I felt like a heel.

"Everything. I remember everything. It just came back to me out of the blue."

"Just now?" He lunged for me and I let him pull me into a hug.

I could have lied to him, but I knew he deserved the truth. "In the kitchen," I mumbled.

"In the kitchen? And you didn't say anything?" I

hated the edge of disappointment in his voice.

"I just freaked out. I didn't know what to say." Talk about understatements.

"How about 'Carter, I remember.'?"

Uh, when he put it like that it seemed like the logical thing to do, unfortunately I was me and I did things my own way. "I'm sorry."

"When were you planning to tell me?"

"I just needed a minute to myself. I was freaking out a little bit." I was planning to tell him right away, wasn't I? I didn't know for sure anymore.

"Did you need the time to dig around for the ring?"

I thought back. No, I had needed time to think, but it was true that left the kitchen knowing I was going to look for it.

"No, well yes. I remembered the ring and I just had to make sure that I was right. But it's not in your drawer anymore so I was worried you had changed your mind. I don't know what happened after that, I just snapped. I *had* to find it. I didn't mean to ruin your surprise, Carter. Really." Snapped. That was what people with temporary insanity pleaded in court.

"I moved it." Well, at least he didn't say he had changed his mind.

"Oh." We stood there awkwardly, which wasn't something that happened to us very often. With Carter at least, I was always in my comfort zone.

"Well, at least you got your memory back. That's what's most important right now." That's right. I had full use of my faculties for the first time in days. It felt wonderful. Except for this situation, of course.

"So, you remember the last two years?" I nodded.

"What about us? Do you remember us?"

"Of course. That's why I hugged you in the kitchen. I was so happy to remember you again." I gave him a big smile and held him to me. "I love you. Thank you for taking such good care of me." He really was the most wonderful man in the world.

"Oh Juss. I love you so much." He leaned down and captured my mouth, his tongue mingled with mine. I felt a zing in my lady parts and I wiggled to relieve some of the pressure.

He continued kissing me as he moved me backwards and toward the bed and I took the few seconds he was turning off the movie to divest myself of my pajama top. Carter turned around, saw me and jerked his own shirt off while I kicked away my pants and panties.

Carter was going too slowly for my taste so I reached over to unsnap his jeans. "Hurry."

He listened to me and unsnapped his jeans, whipping them off in a flash. I took the opportunity to climb up on the bed and kneel in the center. Carter followed me up seconds later. We were pressed together and I could feel the hairs on his legs against my thighs. I didn't resist as Carter pushed me down on the bed with my head on the pillows, I just opened my legs and wrapped them around him. Carter dragged his finger up my slit and I shivered. I needed him desperately.

He bent his head as if her were going to go down on me and I stopped him. "No time. I need you inside me now."

Carter gave me a smile that reminded me of a pirate and positioned himself at my entrance. I was just about to grab his ass and force him inside of me when he did it himself. For a second I felt like I would black out. It felt that good, but I regained my equilibrium a second later as he moved me over and started thrusting in and out of me. It didn't take long for my orgasm to overtake me and the next thing I knew Carter was holding my waist and nudging me.

"Flip over." Now we're talking. It's like he was inside my head and knew just what I needed.

I moved to my hands and knees and let him angle me until I was filled with him again.

"Oh god, Carter. Hard, I need it *hard*." In the next breath he was slamming into me as if his life depended on it. I could barely get enough air my gasps were coming so fast. I lifted one hand and rubbed a circle on my clit, coming apart almost immediately before collapsing down onto my face. I was completely spent. Obviously Carter wasn't. Before I was even able to turn my head to get air, Carter was pulling me up and settling me on his lap. I felt fuller than I had ever been, and as hypersensitive as was humanly possible.

He grabbed me around the waist and moved me on top of him before I took over and ground myself on him. He came almost instantly and pulled us down onto the pillows with a moan. I tried to get my breathing back to normal while Carter moved his hand on my hip. I felt *perfect* in that moment.

"I missed you." His words, spoken into my hair sent a warm thrill through me.

"I missed you, too. I don't ever want to feel so alone again." Thinking back to the strangeness of my amnesia made me feel extra grateful that I remembered how important Carter was to me. He was The One. I knew it in my heart and after my momentary cold feet on Friday and my little flip out a few minutes ago; I now knew it in my head. I wasn't scared anymore.

"We need to talk. About *it*." I would have liked to put it off a little longer and wallow in my happiness and satisfaction, but I sighed. I knew he was right.

Chapter Twenty Three

I wondered if I should talk first and explain my feelings or if Carter was going to break the silence. I knew we had to clear the air, so much had happened, and although I had been a little out of it for the past three days, I was fully in control of my mind now. I felt terrible about what I had put Carter through. Looking at him with full faculties, I could see the strain that my amnesia had had on him. He looked tired and strained, even though he seemed a bit better today than he had been yesterday.

"Well, I guess I'll start." Whew, Carter was going to break the ice on what I knew was going to be a stressful conversation. "How did you find out about the ring?" I scooted out of his arms and turned myself to face him. He didn't look angry so that gave me the confidence to tell him the truth.

"Elisa told me." I was not afraid to throw her under the bus. I would never trust her again. "She just called me out of the blue and I wouldn't have answered normally, but I was just finished uploading my latest post and I was distracted thinking about what dishes I wanted to order for dinner that night at the new Thai place. Once I hit the button I was sorry I had done it, but it was too late. She was talking about going on a date with some guy from work and I was just listening and agreeing with her when she told me she had something to tell me in confidence."

I hesitated to share the rest with Carter. He worked with Elisa and I didn't want him to have conflict at the office, but I knew he deserved the full story. Things with her had gotten out of hand even before she dared to ruin Carter's proposal to me. It seemed like she was trying to sabotage his life.

"She told me that you had told everyone in the office that you had a ring for me and you were going to ask me to marry you. I didn't say anything for a second because I was so caught off guard, but then she went on and said you had something special planned for me. I told her thanks for the info and hung up. I don't know how to explain it Carter, I was here all alone and I just panicked. I thought about the shopping trip that Cheryl had strong-armed me into and it all fit. Then I wondered if Elisa was telling me the truth so I went through your desk, sorry." I felt bad admitting to him how I had invaded his privacy, but he knew that already anyway, so I figured I might as well confess everything.

"When I couldn't find anything there I started going through your drawers, and I must say you don't hide things very well." Carter gave me a look that made me feel about ten years old so I went on. "Anyway, I stood there with the box in my hand and my heart was pounding. I was afraid to open it but at the same time I was excited. When I pulled the top back it felt like my heart stopped. It was the most gorgeous thing I had ever seen. The green of the stone was like the color of your eyes and all I wanted at that moment was to for you to ask me to marry you." I closed my eyes and braced myself to finish.

"But after a minute I started thinking about being married and it just seemed like the most frightening thing in the world." I felt bad when I saw the look on his face. I pulled my hand up to his jaw and let it drift down to his chin. I didn't say anything else, just waited for him to respond to what I'd just told him.

"What are you afraid of?" His voice was quiet. I wanted to be able to tell him that I wasn't afraid anymore but that wasn't true. I wanted to marry him but I was still scared.

"That I won't be the kind of wife you need. You know that I don't have any example of how to be a good wife except your mother, and I am definitely not in the same league as Sharon. I can't entertain people effortlessly like she does, I'm not a good decorator, I mean, since you've moved in my house is the most stylish I've ever seen it. You know me Carter. I say the wrong thing at every opportunity, there's no telling what kind of trouble my mouth will get me into next. The whole reason my web show got so popular was because of all of the dumb crap I say when I go off-script. If we were married, it would reflect on you." I would have gone on but Carter was shaking his head.

"You are the kind of wife I *want*, Justine, and that's all that matters to me. I don't want a clone of my mother. I want *you*. I *need* you." My heart stuttered at his words. They were the most perfect words ever spoken and, oh my god, he was saying them to *me*.

I looked into his eyes and leaned forward to kiss him lightly on the lips. I was expecting him to propose any second. This was the moment most girls dreamed of their entire lives, myself not included, but I was still waiting anxiously.

"Is that why you were acting so weird Friday night?" Those were *so* not the words I had been expecting.

"Well, yeah. I mean, I had just been told a huge secret, which, the more I think about it was incredibly hateful of her, ruining your moment and all, and then I was feeling guilty because I went through all of your stuff and found the ring. I was practically bursting. I was feeling all wound up. Then you came home as relaxed as ever and you weren't acting like you had some big secret then I started second guessing myself." I would have kept on rambling but Carter interrupted me.

"Okay, I get it, but I have to ask, and don't lie to me now, do you think you got the amnesia because you didn't want to marry me?" I opened my mouth to deny it, but he went on. "Seriously Justine, you forgot our entire relationship. You forgot back to before we were ever together." Crap. He sounded so hurt. I guess he had a point. I did forget it all. What did it mean? I didn't know what to say so I stayed silent. Heck, I didn't know why I forgot that particular chunk of my memory, but his explanation sounded reasonable. That made me feel like a lame-o. I liked to think I was a better person than that. God, that's the kind of thing Mom would do. Ugh.

"I'm so sorry Carter. I don't know what else to say. I would never have done that on purpose."

"I know, babe." He sounded like he meant it, but I couldn't be sure. I was wrong pretty often.

"Really, I love you so much. I would *never* want to forget you. You're the most important thing in my life." I grabbed his bicep. Hmm. That's a nice bicep. I shook my head to get back on track. *Focus* Justine. I realized it was time to put it all on the line. I had to let Carter know that I was a sure thing. "You are *it* for me."

He didn't say anything to my declaration, but his face seemed to relax as well as the muscles underneath the hand still clutching his arm. That was a good sign, right?

We looked at each other for what seemed like eternity. I was waiting impatiently for him to ask me, all the while thinking of how I would tell my future children about their father's proposal to me. I was pretty sure I was going to leave the nakedness and post coital bliss part out. I was so wrapped up in my fantasy that I was caught off guard by his next words.

"I'm starving. I'm going to make a sandwich. Do you want me to make you anything?" What the *fuck*? I was lounging here *naked*, waiting for a marriage proposal and he wanted to make a *sandwich*? I sat up in outrage. Maybe I was missing something, but I thought we had just overcome a huge emotional hurdle. I wanted to be held and caressed. Hell, I wanted him to propose, not get up and eat. This wasn't going the way I thought it would at all.

"No, I'm not hungry." I don't know how I managed to keep my voice steady, but it sounded clear and strong, not giving a hint of my jumbled emotions.

I watched as he stood up and grabbed his jeans off of the floor, pulling them on without underwear and leaving the button undone. He walked out, shooting me a smile as he left me alone and confused on the bed. What had just happened here? Hadn't I laid my heart at his feet and admitted that I loved him more than anything else in the world? How could he pass up such a perfect opportunity to ask me? I got up too, pulling my own clothes back on hastily and barreling into the kitchen. He was piling shaved turkey onto his bread as I made my way into the room. He turned around with a smirk.

"Changed your mind about the food?"

"Changed your mind about the proposal?"

Chapter Twenty Four

Oh my god. I wanted to cringe and take the words back, but at the same time I wanted an answer. The look of surprise on Carter's face gave me clue that he may not have been on the same page as me at this moment.

It took him a second but after his initial shock wore off, Carter finally answered. "No, of course I haven't changed my mind."

Whew, the fear I hadn't wanted to acknowledge released its hold on my stomach and suddenly, that sandwich Carter was making looked delicious.

"Well, I changed my mind about the sandwich. I'm hungry."

He smiled and grabbed some more bread out of the bag. "Your wish is my command." Oh how I wished that were true. He would be on one knee in front of me at this very second.

I walked over to stand next to him, pressing myself against his side. I felt like I had been woken from some weird coma in which I could see and hear everything but couldn't really act on anything. I wanted to make up time that I had lost. Actually, I wanted to turn back the clock to Friday and never to have answered Elisa's call. Carter would have proposed to me on Saturday and I would be contentedly wearing that beautiful ring right now. There was no doubt in my mind that I would have told him yes. I only freaked out on Friday because I was left to wallow in my own mind, and that's never a good idea.

I watched Carter build another sandwich, slightly smaller than his own, and marveled again at the fact that I could have forgotten how vital he is to me. I looked up at his profile, taking in his lovely jaw line and his straight nose. I was going to burn his features into my brain so that I would never forget them again. I was ashamed of myself, even if I didn't have total control of my brain's decision to shield me from my stress. Stupid brain. It messed up everything.

I slung my arm around Carter's bare waist and I could feel his muscles quiver. It made my own insides tremble. I felt like a skittish horse, and I hadn't felt this way since the beginning of our relationship, but unlike the beginnings of our relationship, I knew his mind now and didn't have to guess at his feelings. I was confident in his love for me, the trembling was from excitement. I was on the verge of soldering him to me forever.

Carter finished the sandwiches and slid my plate over. Our hands brushed as I picked it up and an electrical current seemed to shoot up my arm and straight to my heart. I carried my plate to the island and sat down while he walked around and sat down next to me. I felt good. I felt right. It seemed that the amnesia gave me the opportunity to have my old life back, and all I tried to do was claw my way back to the present. I realized now that I would never want to go back to the time before Carter was the most important thing in my life. Why would I? I had the life I never even dreamed was possible before.

I took a huge bite of my sandwich while Carter picked up his own. I smiled at him while I was chewing and he smiled back.

"Justine, will you make me the happiest person in the world and marry me?"

What the hell? I swallowed part of what was in my mouth out of pure shock. I started coughing and what was still in my mouth flew out and onto my plate. Carter threw down his own sandwich to slap me on my back. When I got my breath back I looked up at him through my tearing eyes. He was looking at me guiltily and I couldn't have that. I launched myself at him, grabbing him around his neck.

"Yes, yes, yes, yes." His arms reached around to encircle me and for the first time in my entire life I felt like I was truly complete. This was the feeling I had to wait thirty years to feel and it was fucking worth it. I wanted to dance around the kitchen in glee, but I didn't want to let go of Carter's neck just in case the feeling somehow dissipated.

Carter didn't say anything, but I could feel wetness against my cheek. I pulled back slightly so that I could look at his face. Oh my god, he was actually crying.

"Are you all right?" I asked him in a soft voice because my heart had seized up at the sight of his tears.

"I have never been better. I was so scared for the past three days that I had lost you and now everything in my world is perfect. I wouldn't change a thing." He smiled the most brilliant smile and I found myself dazzled by the look in his eyes. My heart wanted to burst in my chest.

I took a deep breath and thought about the one thing that was missing. "Carter, can I have my ring now?" Yeah, I had to break the moment. I wanted that ring on my finger, pronto.

His smile morphed into a smirk as he stood up and grasped my hand, practically dragging me along behind him. He stopped at the closet door and turned on the light, reaching under a stack of jeans and coming back with the familiar little box. I stopped breathing as he dropped to one knee and pulled the ring out. It looked even more breathtaking than before.

"Justine Taylor, will you do me the honor of becoming my wife?" My heart was pounding in my chest and I was rendered speechless at his second, more formal proposal. All I could do was nod frantically and stare as he slipped the ring onto my finger torturously slowly. In the next second I leaned down to him again and grabbed him into a hug that knocked him down and onto the floor of the closet. I fell on top of him and started kissing his face in a frenzy of happiness.

I would have kept kissing him for long minutes, but I wanted to see how the ring looked on my finger. I sat up and held up the ring to the light. It was so magnificent that I turned my hand around in different positions so that I could see it from every angle. It was the loveliest ring I had ever seen and it was all mine, mine, *mine*. I wanted to run outside and shout to all my neighbors that I was marrying the most fantastic man on the planet, but I knew they would probably think I was crazy so I settled for the next best thing.

"I've got to call Cheryl." I announced in my next breath. I stood up and pulled Carter up next to me. "I know she knows you're going to ask me, but I have to tell her *now*."

"That's fine, she would probably be mad if you kept it from her anyway." He grabbed a tee shirt from the closet and pulled it on. I felt a moment's regret that he was covering his glorious body from me but my need to speak to Cheryl overcame everything else.

I looked over to the bedside table and saw only my kisses, iced tea, and my book from the night before.

"Where's my phone?" I wondered aloud.

"It's in the kitchen." He said the words almost guiltily, but I didn't even care as I took off to the kitchen. When I got under the kitchen light the ring sparkled into my eyes almost blinding me with its radiance. I smiled and snatched my phone dialing Cheryl at breakneck speed.

"Justine? Is everything okay? It's late." Oops, in my fever to tell her my news, I forgot to look at the clock. Cheryl and Paulo went to sleep early.

"Carter asked me to marry him. I'm getting *married!*" I practically screamed into phone.

Cheryl's shriek made me pull the phone away from my ear. I could hear her rousing Paulo from his slumber.

She came back down to earth a second later. "Wait. Juss, what about your memory? Did you get it back?"

"Yes Cheryl. I remember *everything*." She

shrieked again and I could imagine her bouncing up and down on her bed. Poor Paulo.

"Oh my god. Oh my *god*. You're really going to be my *sister*. We've got to get planning your wedding. I have so many ideas." Whoa, I needed to slow the Cheryl freight train down and fast.

"Wait. I can't think of any of that right now. It just happened. I just wanted to tell you right away."

"Oh okay. Is my brother with you?"

I turned around and noticed Carter standing beside the refrigerator with a smile. "Yeah he's right here, do you want to talk to him?"

"Please. I'm so happy for you, Juss."

"Okay, I'll talk to you tomorrow." I handed the phone to Carter and sat down on my stool to further admire my new ring. As beautiful as the emerald was, it really didn't hold a candle to Carter's eyes. They were glowing as he looked at me while talking to his sister.

I got up and walked over to him mouthing "Hang up" when I got in front of him.

"Cheryl I've got to go. We'll talk tomorrow." He hit the end button before she could say another word and I took his face in my hands and pulled him down to me.

"I love you so much. I have never felt even close to this wonderful in my whole life." I kissed his lips lightly before I closed my eyes and sunk into him. I could feel myself branding this memory into my psyche forever. My kitchen would be linked to the happiest moment of my life for all time. How fitting.

I felt Lucy's claws digging into my shin and looked down to see her standing on her hind legs waiting to be picked up. She could feel our happiness and wanted in on it. I reached down and scooped her up.

"Mommy and Daddy are getting married. Aren't you excited?" She licked my face in response and I hugged her tighter. I put my other arm back around Carter and we stood in our happy little family unit.

Chapter Twenty Five

The doorbell's incessant ringing was making my soufflé fall during a Food Network Challenge. My god, there was ten thousand dollars at stake, couldn't *someone* get up and answer the damn door? Wait. Huh? I lifted my head and the sparkle from my gorgeous engagement ring caught my eye in the dim light. Oh yeah. My mind was fully alert now, and I could feel the smile stretching the morning-tired muscles of my face. All traces of my dream evaporated as I looked over to Carter and saw him struggling to wake up, too.

"Who the heck would be mashing the doorbell so dang early?" My voice sounded hoarse to my ears.

"One guess. I'm surprised she waited till dawn. She was probably dressed and counting the minutes until she felt it was a reasonable time to come over." Carter stopped talking for a moment and gave me a look so overflowing with love that my stomach fluttered. "Good morning, my lovely fiancée."

I smiled even bigger and threw my left hand out in front of me so that Carter could admire the ring on my finger as well. "Good morning, future husband."

Ooh, that sounds good. Carter was mine. It was pretty much official now, I was wearing this chunk of emerald on my ring finger, and there was no way anybody was going to pry it off.

The next assault on the doorbell started again so I sat up. "Let yourself in, Cheryl," I screeched at the top of my lungs, only belatedly realizing that Lucy was also barking at the front door. A second later the chimes and barking stopped and Cheryl and Lucy came barreling down the hallway together.

"Let me see it!" She bounded up onto the foot of the bed a second before Lucy, bouncing up and down. "Let me see it!"

"You already saw it." Carter was hoisting himself up on one elbow. "It hasn't changed since the last time you looked at it."

"I know, but I want to see it *on.*" I dutifully held up my hand to Cheryl's face. "It's beautiful. Oh my god, Juss, you're really going to be my *sister.*" She leaned forward and grabbed me around the neck for a hug. I threw my arms around her and we squealed for a second before I pulled back.

"I need coffee." I wasn't as groggy as most mornings, surely the result of a fantastic night, but I still wasn't at my best before caffeine.

"I'll make it." Carter pulled himself out of bed and walked out of the room after raising his brow and giving me a suggestive look. Wow, he can make my girly bits zing silently and from across the room. *Impressive.* I gave him a saucy wink in return and he walked out of sight. Cheryl was back to inspecting the ring. She was moving my hand from side to side to try to catch the light from different angles, much as I had done continually last night from the time he slipped it on my finger until I turned off my bedside lamp well after my usual bedtime.

"Okay, he's gone, you can tell me *everything*."

"There's really not much to tell, Cheryl. I got my memory back and then we talked about what happened and then he asked me." I left out the sex because even though Cheryl knew I had sex with her brother, it still weirded me out a little. The Elisa part I left out because it just made me feel bad.

"Details, Justine. I need details. How did he ask you? Where were you? What were you wearing? Were you surprised?"

"Uh, he just asked me. We were in the kitchen eating sandwiches." It didn't seem romantic when I said it, at least not as romantic as it felt.

Cheryl looked confused. "In the kitchen? Did he just pull out the ring and propose in the middle of dinner?"

"He didn't have the ring on him; it was still in the bedroom." Hmm. It was sounded even less romantic upon retelling.

"He didn't have the ring? Was he at least on one knee?"

"Not really. He was on his stool and I was on mine. He asked me and I started choking on my sandwich." Nah, it was still romantic. It was totally us. Me choking was a lot more normal and natural than some over the top proposal surrounded by flowers and candles.

"My brother is such an idiot. I can't believe he didn't do something romantic for you. He had booked a private lake cruise with dinner and everything. He had the whole thing planned out. You would have loved it."

217

I was taken aback by Carter's grand plans. I was infinitely happier with the kitchen proposal in my pajamas. He told me last night that he was overcome with love for me and couldn't hold the words in. That confession made me feel magical. He loved me so much the words just exploded out of him. *He was so much like me.* Sure, he was super-hot and pretty smooth, but he could still dork out occasionally. I don't think I could be with someone who was too cool. It wouldn't be natural.

"No, Cheryl. It was awesome. It was perfect."

"Well, I guess he caught you by surprise if you started choking. Did you even have a *clue*?" I didn't want to tell her about Elisa, but this was Cheryl and she would surely browbeat me until she knew every detail.

"Actually, I knew he was going to ask me. I found the ring on Friday."

"What? Why didn't you tell me? I was trying to be all stealthy by taking you shopping with me to find you the perfect outfit and you knew all along?" Cheryl seemed exasperated that I blew her covert shopping trip.

"I found it after I saw you. Elisa called me and told me Carter had a ring for me." Fresh anger at Elisa's bitchiness flooded through me.

"*What?* That heifer told you and ruined Carter's surprise? Let's go find her and kick her ass. She wouldn't stand a chance against the both of us." I smiled but Cheryl was deadly serious. Cheryl was tons of fun and a ball of energy, but when you crossed her or anyone she loved the gloves came off. She'd cut a bitch.

I was instantly transported to our first month as

roommates and the creepy dude who lived next door to us. She totally beat him with her umbrella when she saw him skulking around our front door for the second time. That guy never gave us another second's problem and moved out after Cheryl told everyone on our street that he was a pervert.

"I know. That was a shitty move wasn't it? I don't know what I've ever done to her to piss her off. I'm nice to her every time I see her. See if she gets invited to one of my dinner parties again." I was so angry that for a second I considered Cheryl's idea. I quickly discarded it when I thought about how mad Carter would be if his sister and fiancée got thrown into jail for assaulting his coworker. Yeah, that was probably too over the top to consider, but she deserved something. I had to put that thought on the back burner when I saw Carter coming back down the hall and veering into the bathroom. A fresh smile bloomed on my face.

"Isn't he dreamy?"

Cheryl rolled her eyes. "Yes, he's the dreamiest. Now, on to the important stuff. I brought a whole stack of wedding magazines and all of my catalogs. Most of the stuff is the same, and it will be a good place to start."

I shook my head. There wouldn't be any stopping her, and I fully intended to sit and pore over every single publication with her, but not without my morning Carter fix. The coffee smelled good and it was calling me, but at this moment, nothing was as important as seeing my fiancé.

"Cheryl, you can bring all those magazines to the kitchen, I need to brush my teeth and get some coffee. I'll meet you in five minutes."

"Okay." She bopped out of the room and I made my way to the bathroom where Carter was wiping water off of his face.

"Hey." He turned toward me and pulled me close to him. "Sorry Cheryl came so early, I had a different morning planned."

"That's okay. I expect she already had everything planned out; she was just waiting for me to say yes so that she could haul everything over here. I'm surprised she didn't bring your mom along."

"Oh, I'm sure she'll be over here before the day is out. Maybe I'll go into work after all." Last night Carter decided that since he had the days off anyway, he'd take advantage of the next few days at home with me.

"Don't you leave me alone with those two. They'll have me choosing between six shades of lilac for centerpieces or something. Besides, you have much better taste than I do." It didn't pain me to admit the truth. Carter was a fashionable dude with an eye for color. I would trust his choices much more than I would my own.

"Are you set on a big wedding?" he asked tentatively.

"Of course not. We've talked about this. I want a fun party, but I'm not into the poofy dress and becoming a Bridezilla over the font of the invitations." The very thought of a big church wedding where everyone would be staring at me was about the last thing I wanted, but Carter came from a pretty big family and Cheryl's wedding had been like a circus. I didn't think I had much hope of a tiny backyard affair.

"I've been thinking since I got up. I'm off, you're

free, let's fly to Vegas and get married today."

"Get serious. Cheryl would kill us if we didn't let her plan our wedding." That was only partially true; she would probably torture us first.

"It's *our* wedding. Our day. We can still let her plan a party. Hell, I'd love a party, but I just want to marry you. I don't care about any of the other stuff."

I really *was* marrying the perfect man. I didn't have to think about it. I was ready to pack my bags right now. "Can we have Elvis marry us?"

"Absolutely. So, are we doing it?"

"Yes! Oh my god. Yes, let's get married today." I jumped up and grabbed his face to pull down to my level. "You've got to tell Cheryl, though." He widened his eyes but didn't protest as I kissed him.

"Deal. I've already called a kennel for the cat. We can drop her by any time after they open at eight. Cheryl can take Lucy home with her. Go pack." He swatted my butt as I turned towards the kitchen for my coffee. I knew Cheryl and Sharon would be disappointed but I could honestly say I had never been so excited. Later on today I would be Justine Ross.

Chapter Twenty Six

"I now pronounce you husband and wife. You may kiss the bride." Elvis had barely gotten the words out before Carter grabbed me up and crashed his lips to mine. Ahh, I'm married. Holy crap, *I'm married!*

I couldn't even concentrate on my first married kiss because I was so wrapped up in the whole "wedding" euphoria.

After Carter and I decided to fly to Vegas, everything seemed to happen in a flash. I had packed my clothes under Cheryl's supervision, but that was after her near meltdown at our plans. Carter and I were able to placate her after we told her she was still free to plan a massive party for us. She took it far better than we were anticipating, but who knows, she may have just put on a brave front for us. I'm certain poor Paulo would be feeling the brunt of her disillusionment with our decision. Oh well, he married her, she was his problem. *I* married a reasonable and thoughtful Ross.

We had kissed Lucy goodbye and Cheryl said she would take care of everything and lock up the house. She even agreed to catch Monique and take her to the kennel for us. We took her up on it and stuffed our carry-on bags with everything we needed for two days in Las Vegas. It was surprisingly less than I was thinking. Carter had called the airline and managed to get us seats on a flight leaving in three hours so we had to haul butt to get to the airport and check in.

The next few hours were a whirlwind, getting a marriage license and driving to the wedding chapel took less time than renting a car at the airport. We were even able to get matching wedding bands onsite. We hadn't even decided which hotel to stay at yet, we were doing everything on the fly. It was perfect.

"Well Mrs. Ross, what do you want to do now?" Carter whispered the words to me as he broke our kiss. I'm *Mrs. Ross*. Instead of doing my usual happy dance in my head, I went ahead and did it for real. I even grabbed Elvis and did a twirl with him while Carter just watched me and chuckled. I figured it was safe to act like the spazz I was since he was legally stuck with me now. I looked down at the thin platinum band snuggled up against my gorgeous engagement ring and felt like the luckiest woman in the world. I needed to ride this feeling and make it pay.

"I want to hit the slots." Okay, it wasn't romantic, but damn it was fun. I wanted to pull some levers and have a few cocktails. I was in Vegas after all.

Carter rolled his eyes but he did it with a smile. "Okay, but let's get a room first."

"Sure honey, I'm flexible. Every hotel has a casino downstairs." I winked at him as he grabbed my hand. We thanked Elvis and went back out to the car.

We ended up staying at the Bellagio because the water show happened to be going on as we drove up the strip. My squealing had Carter turning into the parking lot a few seconds later.

Check-in was completed in minutes and they even upgraded our room when they found out we were freshly married. We hauled our bags up to our room and I found myself less ready to gamble than I thought. I was feeling pretty frisky.

I pulled Carter close as we surveyed the room. "You know, Carter, I think I've changed my mind. I want to see if married sex is any different than what we're used to." He raised his brow and paused as if to check if I was serious before pulling his shirt over his head. I caught the glint of his wedding ring as he moved and my hooha started tingling. He was mine, all mine.

I hurriedly yanked off my own shirt and started to shimmy out of my jeans. Why did I decide to wear skinny jeans today? They were like a second skin and I couldn't shed them as quickly as I wanted to. Carter was gloriously naked before I was able to peel them off, so he graciously helped by popping the snap of my bra for me.

The second his lips grazed my neck I knew there was no time for the bed. I turned around and threw my arms around his neck as he hoisted me up and onto his waist. My bra was still dangling from my arms, but I wasted no time in wiggling myself into position as he moved us up against the wall. Seconds later he was pounding into me and my back was scraping against something hard.

"Ow babe, ow."

"Am I too much for you?"

"No, I think you're grinding me into the light switch." He immediately took a step back and held onto my butt as he moved us to a flatter area.

"Sorry." He looked remorseful and he stopped all movement from his nether regions. I obviously couldn't have that.

"Don't stop. Everything else is perfect." I tried to lift myself up and down on top of him but I was sadly lacking in upper body strength. Luckily he got the message and a second later we were back on. I was extra glad he was still holding me up a minute later because I came faster than I had ever come before. I couldn't even keep my grip on his neck.

"Oh *god*."

"I'm not god, honey," he ground out as he continued to hammer himself into me. He came moments later with a loud growl.

"You are to me." I was barely able to get the words out I was breathing so hard, but he heard them because his arms tightened and he pressed me harder against the wall.

"I love you, Mrs. Ross." The sound of my new name gave me fresh goosebumps.

"I love you, Mr. Ross." He kissed the tip of my nose before setting me back down on my feet. "Now, get your clothes back on, Double Diamonds is calling my name."

"Is there not a drop of sentimental blood flowing through you right now?" he asked while shaking his head. I could tell he wasn't mad so I didn't feel bad.

"No, I've got gambling fever, now hurry up." I opted for a different pair of jeans, comfort was my goal, but I did put my white blouse back on. It *was* my wedding day.

He dressed almost as fast as he had undressed, so after I checked my appearance in the bathroom mirror we were ready to go.

"Let's go lose some money," he said while taking my hand and leading me out the door.

"Are you kidding me? I'm on the luckiest streak of my life."

EPILOGUE

Hot Buns
(or *How I Got My Cooking Show on TV*)

"That was the coolest thing *ever*! I wish we could have stayed up there all day."

"It was fun I guess, after I got over the nausea," Carter mumbled as we made our way back to the rental car.

I wanted to feel guilty for begging him to go up in the hot air balloon, but *come on*, we were staying in Napa. What romantic trip would be complete without a balloon ride over the vineyards? The fact that Carter went along with it, considering his fear of heights, made me especially glad I had the good sense to marry this wonderful man.

"When we get back to the vineyard I'll show you just how much I appreciate you forfeiting your relaxing morning by spending it up in the sky." I wagged my eyebrows suggestively so that he knew a blow job was in his immediate future.

"I'm actually going to hold you to that." He smirked as we crawled into the car. Yes, getting my way with him was just that easy. We had driven in silence for about a mile when I heard my phone ding out that I had gotten a text. I reached back into my purse and pulled out the phone, thankful that I had left it in the car. How irritating it would have been to hear my phone while we were floating in relative silence.

"Wow. Seven missed texts and four missed calls from Cheryl. What in the world could be so important?"

I opened my texts and felt my body chill as her texts got increasingly more urgent.

OMG! I think there's a problem with your site.

Call me as soon as you get this!

Pull down your new video!!

Call me NOW!!

Where are you?—EMERGENCY

Check your site—hurry!!

You posted a PORN of yourselves on your website!!!!

I pulled up the site and clicked on the most recent update, Hot Cross Buns. We had set two new segments to post automatically while we celebrated our first anniversary in Napa Valley, Hot Cross Buns and Ultimate Mac and Cheese. Unfortunately, what opened was the sex tape we had made after coming home from Cheryl and Paulo's Halloween party. We had been a little tipsy, so filming ourselves had seemed like a good idea at the time. I saw myself doing a drunken striptease while wearing my Princess Leia buns as Carter lounged on the bed wearing nothing but his Jedi belt and a lecherous smile.

"Nooooooo! Carter, we posted our porno on the website!" I could barely get the words out because I could feel myself starting to hyperventilate. Carter screeched to a stop on the shoulder of the road and grabbed the phone out of my now numb fingers.

"Fuck! Why didn't I double check?" He started punching something into the phone while I let the magnitude of this horror sink in. What if it got linked to YouTube? How could I ever show my face again? I had just sent porn to at least six thousand people, not to mention the number of visitors that just happen upon my site by chance while looking for a recipe. I dug out my Xanax and popped one. A few seconds later I shook out another and chewed them both, bitter taste be damned.

"How did it get on our uploads? Were we hacked?" It seemed like the only reasonable explanation.

"No, I named our Halloween tape *Hot Buns* because you looked so sexy in them. I didn't know then that you were going to do a segment on hot cross buns. I just didn't pay enough attention when I was getting everything ready for our trip. I'm so sorry, babe." He wasn't looking at me but at the screen. "It's pretty damn sexy, though."

"Are you kidding me right now? Pull it down before it goes viral!" I couldn't believe he was being such a *man*. Couldn't he see the big picture?

He had the grace to flush. "Right." He typed in a few more things before handing back the phone. "It won't let me log on to the site from the phone; I need to get to the computer." He peeled out and off of the shoulder of the road and sped the six miles back to the Black Dog Winery, while I sat in a semi-shocked stupor, remembering all of the dirty things I had done for the camera. I had another chilling thought.

"What if your mom sees this? Oh god, I'll never be able to look her in the eye again."

"I'm more concerned about the fact that we sent

229

out an adult video without a warning. We could be in a lot of trouble. There are going to be some complaints." Crap. I hadn't even thought of the legal repercussions. They might shut my site down. My vision started to flicker as I let this new information filter in. My dreams of a cooking empire were over. Just when I thought I was home free, with my cookbook out, selling better than expected, and the site getting almost a million hits a month. Why couldn't things ever go smoothly for an extended period? It seemed like there was always something that had to go wrong.

I jolted when the car came to a stop and Carter threw open the car door before hopping out and taking off for our room. I grabbed my stuff out of the back seat and followed at a more leisurely pace. There wasn't anything I could do about it; I let Carter handle the computer stuff.

"Is everything all right, Mrs. Ross? Your husband just came running by." Suzy at the desk was eyeballing me curiously.

"He has an emergency at work." I smiled weakly and continued up to our room. When I opened the door Carter was already at the computer and typing furiously. A few seconds later he looked up.

"I pulled it off of the site, but I can't do anything about the people who already opened their emails. There's already over fifty comments and they aren't flattering."

I took offense at that. Carter and I made a pretty hot couple. We knew what we were doing in bed and we looked good doing it. "What do they say?" I waited a moment but he didn't answer me.

"You had better look for yourself." He scooted

over and patted the bed as my phone rang in my hand. Cheryl.

"Hello?"

"Omigod. Did you get my messages? I've been trying to get in touch with you all morning."

"Yeah. We were on a balloon ride and we left our phones in the car. I'm freaking out, but he's already pulled the video."

"Thank goodness. Mom called and told me to check my email. I think one of her friends saw it and told her about it."

My worst fears were being realized. Not only had Sharon seen our sex tape, but so did any number of people we know.

"Don't tell me anymore, Cheryl, I can't take it. Carter thinks we might get in trouble for sending out an adult movie without a warning. My career is over. I'll never be able to face people again."

"It'll be okay, Juss. Think of what a sex tape did for all those celebrities. They became way more popular than before. Heck, it pretty much made them household names."

"They weren't doing an almost family friendly cooking show! Children watch my program."

"Hmm. I hadn't thought of that. That's actually pretty bad."

"No duh. I'm ruined." I threw myself back onto the bed and closed my eyes. "You didn't watch it did you?"

"Well, let's just say it was nothing I haven't seen before." I cringed at the reminder.

"I'll talk to you later, okay? This is just too much to take in right now and it's my anniversary."

"Oh yeah. Happy Anniversary!" She sounded so

excited that the last few minutes of my life might never have happened. "What are you guys planning for tonight?"

"We're going to have dinner delivered to our terrace, and I'm glad we already booked room service. I just don't think I can face anyone right now."

"There's nothing more you can do about it now, so try to have a good rest of your day. Tell Carter I said hi. Love you."

"Love you too. I'll call you tomorrow. Thanks for letting us know what was going on."

We hung up and I looked over at Carter. "She thinks it will make me famous." He set the computer on the night stand and flopped down onto his back beside me.

"It's my fault. I'll take the blame. I should have been more thorough, but I was excited to get out of town. I've sent out an apology to all of our subscribers, I just hope it's enough to tamp down the outrage. I'm sure you're going to lose a few followers, but you'll probably gain a few more, too. I don't want to think about it right now. I look ridiculous in that footage."

I didn't know how I was going to put it out of my mind, but I was determined to try if only to make our anniversary special. "You and your Princess Leia fetish. Now I don't think I want to pull out the buns."

"You brought 'em?" He perked up immediately. Pervert.

"Yeah, but I don't know if I'll ever be able to wear them without thinking about broadcasting my naked butt to anyone with an internet connection."

"I like your naked butt. Anyway, we'll find out

what the fallout of our movie is soon enough. I think you should go put on your buns and take off everything else. We've got some Anniversary Sex that needs to commence."

"You know what? You're right. And the Xanax has kicked in, so you're in luck." I leaned over him and gave him a kiss. Tomorrow I might be infamous, but I was going to make our anniversary unforgettable.

A Peek Into the Mind of Carter Ross

Love at First Sight

Ten Years Ago

"Carter, hurry up and take out the trash. I'm trying to get this kitchen cleared up before Cheryl and her friend get here."

"I'm coming. Just a minute." I had to yell through the bathroom door because I was still fixing my hair. Nothing I did could tame the wild mess that grew out of my head. I didn't understand it. Neither of my parents was cursed with this shaggy black mane. I had let Cheryl experiment with her straightening iron last summer and although I liked the results it just seemed a little bit too gay to do to myself every morning before school. I ran my fingers through it one more time before giving up and I smiled at myself with an open mouth. I had just gotten my braces off last week and I still liked to check myself out without seeing shiny metal.

I walked down the stairs in no hurry. It wasn't that I was lazy or anything, but Mom was racing around like Cheryl was bringing Princess Diana over or something. I didn't get the big deal. It wasn't as if Cheryl lived across the country and only came home for holidays. She lived in the dorms at UT. We saw her all the time. Too much if you asked me. I was finally in high school and I liked being the only kid in the house. For the first time in my life I didn't have to fight anyone over the Fruity Pebbles and make do with the crappy bran cereal my parents ate or try to get to the Oreos before Cheryl commandeered them to eat in her bedroom with her pack of friends.

I entered the kitchen and saw my mother at the stove stirring a huge pot of *something*. It didn't smell *too* bad, so that was a good sign. I walked over to peer over her shoulder and repressed a shudder. Whatever it was didn't look very appetizing.

"What's that?" I tried to swallow my disappointment at the fact my mother was cooking which automatically ruled out pizza.

"Chili." The watery mess in the pot was supposed to be chili?

"Mmm." I loved my mother with all my heart, but she just could not cook. I figured the nicest thing to say was nothing so I just moved along and grabbed the bag of garbage and carried it outside to the can. I had just closed the lid when Cheryl's Jetta came barreling up the driveway. She screeched to a stop and jumped out.

"Hey Carter, did ya miss me?"

"I just saw you last weekend. I haven't even had a chance to yet." Actually, I did kinda miss her. It was still a little bit strange not to be able to walk across the hall and talk to her if I wanted to. We had always been close and the fact that she was four years older than me meant that we were too far apart in age to get into all of the normal sibling arguments. She came up to me and gave my arm a squeeze. I looked over to her car as I saw the passenger door open.

"Justine, this is my brother Carter." The girl getting out of the car looked over the roof at us and it felt like I got the wind knocked out of me. I met the eyes of the hottest girl I had ever seen.

"Hi Carter. Cheryl has told me all about you." Her voice. Holy crap it was sexy.

I wanted to tell her hello, but my mouth refused to work. I ended up nodding at her stupidly before turning on my heel and walking back into the house. I realized I probably seemed rude, but this was the first time I had ever come face to face with such a gorgeous woman. I opened the back door and walked quickly past my mom.

"Cheryl is here," I managed to say as I made my way back to the stairs and to the sanctuary of my bedroom. When I got there I flopped down on my bed cursing myself for being such a pussy. What the hell is wrong with me that I couldn't even talk to a hot girl? I had to snap out of it immediately and try to reclaim some coolness. I was in high school now; I couldn't let myself look like a fool.

I stood back up and walked over to my closet. The first order of business was to change out of my sweats and into something that made me look more mature. I pulled out some jeans and a blue sweater. I kicked off my sneakers and sweats and hastily pulled on my jeans. I left my tee shirt on and put the sweater on over it. It didn't hurt to bulk up a little bit. I pulled my sneakers back on because I didn't want to look like I was trying too hard and I tried to smooth down my hair. I was going to go back down and impress...shoot, I don't remember what Cheryl called her. Damn it. Now I was going to look stupid if I asked her name. I shook my head and started back down to the kitchen. I could hear the females talking so I straightened up before walking into the room.

"There you are. Are you okay sweetie? Cheryl said you were acting strangely outside." I gave Cheryl a glare before answering.

"I'm fine. I just remembered something and I had to take care of it before I forgot." Whew. My voice had recovered and I sounded coherent. Cheryl looked me over and raised her brow. I should have realized she would notice that I changed clothes. Luckily she didn't say anything out loud, though.

"Well, I hope everybody is hungry. Justine, I made chili in honor of your visit." Justine, her name is Justine. Thanks Mom.

"I certainly am. Thank you for going to all this trouble for me, Sharon." Justine was the only one of us to express her feelings of hunger. Cheryl and I knew mom's cooking for what it was. Practically inedible. Mom pulled some bowls down from the cabinet and started doling out portions.

"Not much for me, Mom. I'm not that hungry." I was starving but I would come back later and make a sandwich or something. I wasn't going to sit here and try to choke down the "chili" in front of Cheryl's friend. I wanted to look smooth in front of her and there was no way to do that while eating mom's cooking.

"Me either. I didn't know you were cooking and I ate some Twinkies before we left." Cheryl knew the drill, too. Poor Justine was going to be taken off guard by mom's food.

We all sat down at the kitchen table and I took the opportunity to grab a handful of shredded cheese to dilute the chili taste. When I looked down at my bowl it was easily two thirds cheese. Perfect.

I was trying to watch Justine out of the corner of my eye. She was so pretty that it was making me act unnaturally.

"So Carter, what grade are you in?" Oh no, she was talking to me directly. I tried to look nonchalant as I met her eyes.

"I'm a freshman." I thought that sounded better than saying ninth grade.

She smiled at me and I could feel myself blushing. Geez, this had never happened with Cheryl's other friends. Okay, that wasn't entirely true, Heather was pretty hot, but she didn't have anything on Justine. She was like a goddess.

"So Justine, what's your major?" My mom stepped into the breach left by my embarrassed silence.

"English. I want to write but I didn't want to go into Journalism. I really wanted to go to cooking school but my mother insisted that I go to a "real" school." She made air quotes around the word real and rolled her eyes, so I figured she didn't agree with her mother's assessment of her educational choices.

"Well, I'm glad you came to UT, otherwise I wouldn't have met you." Cheryl piped in while stirring her bowl. No one but Mom had taken a bite yet. Maybe Cheryl had alerted Justine in advance. I hoped so; it didn't seem fair to make a guest eat this food without forewarning.

Justine smiled and took a bite. She kept smiling as she chewed her mouthful. I looked at Cheryl and she winked at me. Good, that meant Justine knew what was up and was being polite. It made her that much cooler to me.

We sat there chatting and "eating" for about half an hour more before I got up. It was almost time for me to go to my friend Jeff's house. Crud. It had seemed like a good idea to make plans to be out of the house tonight when Cheryl said she was bringing a friend, but now I was mad at myself. I wished I could make up a reason to stay home but his mom was taking us to a movie.

"Well, I have to go. Mom, can I have some money for a movie?" It sucked that I had to ask my mother for cash in front of Justine, but I didn't have anything left after I spent my money on my new telescope. I was actually kicking myself about that purchase since I lived in Austin and the sky was drowned out by all of the light.

"You can grab a twenty out of my purse. Do you want me to drive you?" God, this was getting worse by the minute. Now mom was pointing out that I was too young to drive. I needed to get out of here before I looked like even more of a kid to Justine.

"Nah, I'm good." I walked over to mom's purse and grabbed out a twenty dollar bill before stuffing it in my front pocket.

"Bye Carter, see you later." Cheryl got up to hug me so I hugged her back.

"It was nice meeting you, Carter." Justine's smooth voice made my name sound like a caress. I think I'm in love.

"You too. Bye Mom." I walked out the back door and into the garage to get my bike. I hopped on and took off to ride the four blocks to Jeff's house. I had just met my dream girl. I just hoped Cheryl would stay friends with her so that I would have a chance to get to know her better. Next time I would be ready with some intelligent conversation and possibly some witty banter. As I got closer to Jeff's house I peddled faster; I could hardly wait to tell him about Justine.

Tonight Was the Night

Tonight was the night. I was going to ask Justine out. On a date. My palms started sweating as I waited for her web page to upload. I needed to remind her to upgrade her DSL speed; this slow shit was irritating. Okay, focus man. I took a deep breath to calm my nerves but it didn't work. I was a nervous wreck and I felt like I was sixteen and asking Rachelle Browne to go to the movies on my first real date after I got my driver's license. No, scratch that, this was much harder than when I was a teenager. I liked Justine way back then, when she was so far out of my league as a junior in college, that I would never have dared to ask her out. I really didn't know how I was going to have the cojones to go through with it tonight, though I felt under pressure since her website was finished and with it my reason for coming over here and helping her.

I had to believe that I wasn't going to get shot down right off the bat. I had caught her staring at me a few times and then blushing. I knew when a woman was into me, I hadn't gotten to be twenty four without my fair share of female companionship. I mean, lets be realistic, the ladies thought I was hot. Hell, I bet even dudes thought I was hot, in a non-gay way, of course. I'm not conceited, but I do have eyes. I wasn't sure if that was going to be enough to sway

Juss, though.

I had actually been stealthily trying to worm my way into her consciousness for the past several weeks; standing in her personal space, making comments that were just shy of being innuendos, and most of all, making sure she could see me outside of the realm of "Cheryl's little brother" when possible.

The timing was perfect. She had finally seen her ex for the douchey prick he was and kicked him to the curb a few months ago, thereby leaving the path clear. It was like a sign when she called me up and asked me to help her set up a website. Thank you, Cheryl. Now, it was all up to me.

Upload Complete. So that was it. My work for her was done. I half considered telling her there was some kind of problem, allowing me at least one more official visit, but I just couldn't do that to her. She was really excited about her website idea and I was interested in seeing where she was going to take it. Also, that would have been a really dick move on my part and not the way I wanted to start off a possible relationship. The time was at hand.

I stood up and stretched. I could smell the chicken pot pie she was making for us tonight, part of her payment for my web design services. My stomach rumbled, but unfortunately it was nerves and not hunger. Well, it was hunger too, but mostly it was the fact that I was trying to gather up all of my mojo for the task at hand. I refused to wimp out. Go out there, pussy. I mentally flipped my inner voice the bird and started for the kitchen, slowing my steps as I came around the corner. Justine was standing with her back to me, slicing a cucumber and singing a song that I didn't recognize. I stood there for a minute watching her until I decided to make some noise to alert her to my presence.

I cleared my throat and she spun around holding the knife out in front of her.

"Geez Carter, you scared me." Her cheeks got pink but she smiled at me. "The food is just about ready. How is it going in there?"

"All done. You obviously need to check it over before it goes live, but I've done everything we talked about. It looks great."

She beamed at me with delight. "I'm so excited. I can't thank you enough for this, Carter. I could never have gotten this done without you."

"It was my pleasure. The food has been well worth it. I'm going to miss all of these home cooked meals."

She just smiled at me and blushed before turning back to her cucumber.

It was now or never. "So I was wondering if you wanted to go out with me?" She turned back to me a couple of seconds later.

"Go out?" Uh oh, I could tell she was trying to buy time before answering me.

"Yeah, you know, to dinner or something."

"Um. Well, I work most nights."

"I know. I was thinking maybe next Monday. I'm finished with your site and I know Mondays are your off days. I thought that instead of you having to cook we could go out. Then, maybe we could catch a movie or whatever." I had to admit that my invitation didn't sound very smooth or well thought out, but I had to hope she would overlook that and want to spend time with me anyway.

"Just you and me?"

I nodded.

"You mean a date?"

"Well, yeah." Did I not make myself clear enough?

"I don't know, Carter. That would be kind of weird, you know?"

She was turning me down. To be honest, it didn't occur to me that she would really say no. It took a second for my mind to recognize the feeling in my stomach as disappointment.

My brain went straight into high gear. I knew she liked me, so I had to make her see the benefits of an actual date.

"Why would it be weird? We've known each other for years. We've been spending every Monday evening together for three weeks and there hasn't been any awkwardness."

"That's not the same as a date." She held her hand up as I opened my mouth to protest. "You're Cheryl's brother. That *is* making things awkward. Plus, I'm too old for you."

"You're not too old for me, Justine, that's ridiculous. We're not in high school. We're both adults. I really like you." Shit. That did sound a little bit high school.

"Carter, don't take this the wrong way, but you're too young for me."

Was it possible to take it the right way? I was stuck for a reply to that. I had nothing.

"I really like you, too, though." She started blushing so I jumped on the only chance I was going to get.

"Alright, let's take age out of the equation for a minute. We like each other and we know we get along. What harm could there be in going out for a friendly date and seeing where things might go from there?"

"What about Cheryl?"

"What about her?" Cheryl was the one person in the world who knew that I've always carried a torch for Justine. She used to tease me about it when I was younger, but I didn't think that she would have too much of a problem with the idea of Justine dating me. At least I hoped not.

She raised her brow. "Don't be dense. She would not be cool with it." She didn't say anymore, but bent down to get the pot pie out of the oven. My stomach growled, reminding me that I'd skipped lunch so that I could finish the design on the energy bar wrapper for Breast Cancer Awareness Month. I didn't want to have to work on it tonight since this was my last night working for Justine.

She set the casserole between us on the island and looked at me. "I'm sorry, Carter."

I could tell by her voice that she had decided that a date wasn't going to happen. I had to quickly restrategize.

"What if we stayed in? I'll even cook for you." Did I sound too desperate?

She stared at me for a few seconds more and I could almost hear the crickets chirping. I felt my stomach sink. This sucked.

"I'll cook." What? She was saying yes? I could feel my heartbeat speed up. She wanted to date me! I felt like skipping around the room, and if I was alone I would have, but I wasn't going to do anything to mess this up.

"Great." I made sure my voice was clear and

confident.

"Okay, next Monday we can have some dinner and take it from there. Now, I have to finish the salad."

Her face had turned a little bit pink with embarrassment, so I let her turn around and get back to her cucumber while I mentally gave myself a high five. I was going to make next Monday a night she would never forget.

The Big Unveiling

I was *this* close to shooting my load, but I was trying to make it good for Justine. This was only the third time we'd been together, so I wanted to impress her with my longevity.

"Oh god, oh god." She was panting and grabbing onto my shoulders so I knew she was about to have another orgasm. I increased my tempo, and my breath sounded loud in my own ears. That's probably the reason I didn't hear the door opening until it was too late.

"Oops. Sorry." Jesus, was that *Cheryl*? I turned my head to the voice and met my sister's eyes. "Arrrrgh! Oh my *god*! What's going on?"

"Uhhhgh." I let out a scream of my own, but it wasn't quite as high pitched. A moment later Justine squealed too.

"Fuck Cheryl, can't you *knock*?" I was trying to be a gentleman and cover Justine, but in the process I was exposing more of myself.

"Carter, what the fuck?" Cheryl made a face at my nakedness but didn't move.

"Cheryl, turn around." Justine was frantically trying to disentangle herself from me as Cheryl continued to gape at us.

"Damn Cheryl, take a picture." I gave her my

247

meanest look but she just turned from my eyes to Justine.

"How long has this been going on?" she asked Justine accusingly. Shit, this is just what Justine had been afraid of. This was going to undo all of the progress I had made in getting Justine comfortable with a relationship between us.

"Oh my god." It wasn't the same god she had been chanting to a minute ago. She was bright red and had a look of total horror on her face. This wasn't good at all.

"Cheryl, would you please give us a minute here?" I tried to sound reasonable but the words came out harshly. I loved my sister but she had just created a nightmare scenario for me. She didn't say anything but walked through the living room and into the kitchen. Just great. She wasn't even going to let us get dressed in privacy. This was getting worse by the second.

"I *knew* this was a bad idea. I'm sorry Carter, but we can't be together this way. I told you this wouldn't work."

"Wait. Don't say that. This was just a surprise for us all." I wanted to be the voice of reason but I could feel Justine slipping away from me.

"No Carter. Cheryl wasn't merely surprised she was horrified." She had me there but I wasn't about to give up without a fight. I had waited too long for a chance with her to let it all go now.

I pulled on my jeans and grabbed my tee shirt off of the coffee table. "Please Justine, give me a minute with Cheryl, okay." She nodded because I'm sure she wasn't ready to face the coming inquisition. I got up and stalked into the kitchen like a warrior ready to do battle. Cheryl was standing by the kitchen window.

"I need to talk to you. Outside." I grabbed her by the arm and dragged her to the back door with me. I didn't need Justine overhearing anything that I was about to say to my sister. Cheryl didn't say anything until we were on the patio.

"How could you, Carter? She's my best friend; you can't go around having sex with my friends, that's just gross."

"Cheryl, you know I love you, but you need to butt out. This is between me and Justine."

"You made it about me when you decided to use my best friend for your little romp." She had her hands on her hips and she was giving me her best imitation of our mother's scowl.

"This isn't a romp and you know it. Don't try and pretend you don't know how I feel about her. You've always known." Her face softened slightly but she wasn't ready to let me off the hook just yet.

"Carter, this isn't the same thing as you mooning around after my roommate. We're all adults now and this could get really complicated. I don't want to see her get hurt. You either." She had said the last part almost grudgingly.

"The only thing that will hurt me now is if you say or do something that makes Justine decide that being with me is wrong." I reached out and took her hand. "Please Cheryl; help me make things right with her." I was practically pleading with her at this point but it was my now or never moment. She gave me a searching look but I could see I was getting through to her.

"Promise me this isn't some passing thing with

you. This isn't another Christina?"

I cringed inwardly at the reminder of Christina. She was pretty and she was cool to hang out with, but I had used her to make myself feel better after seeing Justine with that creep John who she had started dating. My parents had thrown a dinner party and I knew Justine was bringing that putz so I invited Christina along. Big mistake. She had been under the impression that she was "meeting the parents" and I had compounded the problem by behaving as if we were much more of a couple than we were. After she started getting a little bit too attached, I broke up with her as nicely as possible. That didn't stop her from calling me with a stalkerish frequency or showing up at Cheryl's house hoping that my sister would be able to change my mind.

"You know that whole business with Christina was directly related to Justine. Come on, how often do I ask anything from you? Never, so please, please go in there and tell her you don't have a problem with us being together. Even if you do, do it for me. I *love* her, Cheryl."

She looked at me speculatively. "How long have you and she been..." She gestured between me and the house.

"For almost a month." I ignored the look of surprise on her face. "Really, since I started helping her with her website. She's awesome."

"I know she is. That's why I don't want you to do anything to mess her up. She's important to me."

"She's important to me too. *Please.*" I was full on begging.

"Okay Carter. I'm going to go in there and tell her I was just surprised and that I think you're a great guy and she should give you a chance. But," she leaned over and poked me in the chest with her finger. "If you do anything to hurt her or in any way mess up *my* friendship with her because of this, I'm going to Fuck. You. Up." She punctuated each word with and extra hard poke. "Are we clear?" This was the meanest I had seen Cheryl since we were kids and I cut off the hair of her favorite Barbie doll so I knew she meant business.

"Crystal. Thanks, I owe you big."

"Don't worry; you'll be paying up when the time is right." Without another word she walked back into the living room, leaving me to wonder what was going on inside Justine's head.

I Am a Knight

"Aaiigh! Help!" Justine's scream ripped through the house just as I was pulling my boxers on after my shower. I tore through the distance between the bedroom and the kitchen in record time. That was the "I just cut my pinky finger off" kind of scream. I arrived to the sight of Juss standing hunched over on the island with a dish towel in one hand and a spatula in the other.

"What are you doing? What's the matter?"

"There's a *rat* in here. I just saw it run into the laundry room."

I pulled out the old standby phrase. "It's more scared of you than you are of it."

"That's bull! There is *no way* it's more scared than I am."

"Where did it come from?"

"Somewhere behind me. I saw it run along the baseboards and under the laundry room door. *Go get it!*"

Fuck. The last thing I wanted to do right now was catch a rat, but we couldn't have one loose in the house. I shuddered at the thought of coming face to face with such nasty vermin. How the hell did we get a rat in here? We'd never had a rodent problem before. Juss was adamant about keeping those "pesta-way" things plugged in at all times. It must have crawled through the doggy door. But in broad daylight? It probably had rabies. I didn't share that with Justine; I wanted her to come down some time today.

"I'll go get something to catch it with." I immediately thought of my old lacrosse stick from high school. It had a net on the end and it was long, keeping me from having to get too close to any rodent. I dug it out from the back corner of the office closet before making my way back down the hallway, feigning some of my old moves. Yeah, I still had it going on.

"Hurry up!" she barked at me.

Apparently, Justine wasn't a lacrosse fan. As I got closer, I could see she was shaking. She was so lucky she had me to do these kinds of things for her. I didn't want to say it out loud, but rats scared the crap out of me, too.

I looked over at Justine and held my finger to my lips in the universal sign of "be quiet," then held the stick in front of me as a weapon while I crept over to the door and turned the handle.

I threw back the door and burst into the laundry room, but I couldn't get a bead on it. I tiptoed stealthily over to the washer and dryer and leaned over to see which machine it was hiding behind. Nothing.

"It's not in here, babe. Are you *sure* you saw one?" She turned on me in outrage.

"Of course I did! Would I scream for you otherwise? Find it and *kill it*."

"I'm not going to kill it. I'm strictly catch and release." Just then I saw a movement to my left and

253

instinctively swung the stick toward it, capturing the beast for my love. A split second later a tiny field mouse shot through the mesh of the stick and back into the kitchen.

"There it is! There it is!" Justine was screaming and pointing to the wall so I yanked the back door open, allowing it to escape into the grass. I turned around to receive my praise, but found Justine collapsed on the island, shaking uncontrollably.

"Are you okay? Baby, talk to me. It was only a little mouse." She didn't say anything for a few seconds, but she suddenly burst into laughter.

"You looked *hilarious*. Omigod, first you were posing and then you were stalking it, and your wiener was hanging out the *whole time*." She took a deep breath, only to start cackling again.

I looked down and saw that my dick was poking out of the flap in the front of my boxer briefs.

"You think my wiener looks funny, do you?" I put on the most menacing look I could muster as said wiener took it upon itself to stiffen and enlarge.

"Yes, but maybe I just need to see it up close."

Oh yeah, now I was going to get my reward. "By all means, check it out." I stifled a groan as she scooted off of the island and stood in front of me, grasping my cock between her fingers.

"Hmm. It looks much more sinister up close, but I need to be sure." She dropped to her knees in front of me, pulling my boxers down and over my, now huge, erection.

"I don't hear any laughing." I stiffened as she leaned forward and enveloped my dick with her lips.

"Nnnmmn," she hummed, sending a shock wave through my body. She pulled back, making a popping sound as she released my rod from her mouth. "It appears I was mistaken. It's actually quite intimidating." She stayed where she was and looked up at me. "What can I do to repay you for your act of bravery?"

I felt like a knight (a Jedi one) who just won the hand of a fair maiden.

"You were off to a pretty good start." A second later she cupped my balls with one hand and used the other to grip my ass and pull me closer to her head. *Yes!* If this was how she wanted to thank me for ridding our house of pests, I vowed to jump to attention the next time she squealed at a spider in the bathtub.

I had to restrain myself from thrusting my hips and shoving my cock farther down her throat; for some reason that really pisses her off. I gasped as she scraped her teeth lightly up my shaft. Damn, I was already about to blow, but I wasn't ready for it to be over, yet. "Stop. I need a second."

"It's now or never. Your parents will be here any minute and you still need to get dressed." Oh yeah, that's what I'd been doing when she'd screamed. I'd better let her finish me off, then.

No sooner had I had the thought, then the damn doorbell started ringing. *Motherfucker! Why?*

Justine shrugged and pulled my underwear up before standing. "Sorry."

"Not as sorry as I am." The bell pealed again.

"Coming," Justine called as she walked toward the front door, leaving me to sprint to the bedroom to finish dressing. It took a couple of minutes before my cock deflated to a size suitable for company.

By the time I came out of hiding, Mom and Dad

were sitting on the stools in the kitchen while Justine slid a tray of onion tartlets in front of them. Dad looked over his shoulder at me and wagged his eyebrows. He somehow knew what he'd interrupted. *Cockblocker!* I sent him a glare and continued into the kitchen. The sooner we ate, the sooner this evening would be over and we could get back to the important stuff.

Don't miss other Genevieve Jourdin titles from
Pin-up Press

Baby, It's Cold Outside (Fire & Ice Book 2)

PreHeat (Fire & Ice Book 0) Prequel
Novelette

Late Night Snacks 4 Story Bundle

Awake

Journal of a Jaded Housewife

Visit me at **Genjourdin.com** or email me at

Genjourdin@gmail.com

www.ingramcontent.com/pod-product-compliance
Lightning Source LLC
Chambersburg PA
CBHW031713170626
46808CB00005B/1732